year of
mistaken
discoveries

Also by

EILEEN COOK

What Would Emma Do?

Getting Revenge on Lauren Wood

The Education of Hailey Kendrick

Unraveling Isobel

Used to Be

The Almost Truth

Remember

year of
mistaken
discoveries

EILEEN COOK

SIMON PULSE

NEW YORK   LONDON   TORONTO   SYDNEY   NEW DELHI

SIMON PULSE
An imprint of Simon & Schuster Children's Publishing Division
1230 Avenue of the Americas, New York, NY 10020
This Simon Pulse paperback edition January 2015
Text copyright © 2014 by Eileen Cook
Also available in a Simon Pulse hardcover edition.
All rights reserved, including the right of reproduction in whole or in part in any form.
SIMON PULSE and colophon are registered trademarks of Simon & Schuster, Inc.
For information about special discounts for bulk purchases, please contact
Simon & Schuster Special Sales at 1-866-506-1949 or business@simonandschuster.com.
The Simon & Schuster Speakers Bureau can bring authors to your live event.
For more information or to book an event contact the Simon & Schuster Speakers Bureau at
1-866-248-3049 or visit our website at www.simonspeakers.com.
Cover photograph copyright © 2014 by Marcus Noessing/Corbis
Cover designed by Karina Granda
Interior designed by Angela Goddard
The text of this book was set in Adobe Garamond.
Manufactured in the United States of America
2 4 6 8 10 9 7 5 3 1
The Library of Congress has cataloged the hardcover edition as follows:
Cook, Eileen.
Year of mistaken discoveries / Eileen Cook.— First Simon Pulse hardcover edition. pages cm
Summary: Partnered with a boy named Brody, high school senior Avery embarks on a class
project to find her birth mother, after Avery's former best friend, also adopted, dies.
ISBN 978-1-4424-4022-7 (hc) — ISBN 978-1-4424-4024-1 (eBook) —
ISBN 978-1-4424-4023-4 (pbk)
[1. Friendship—Fiction. 2. Adoption—Fiction. 3. Birthmothers—Fiction.
4. Dating (Social customs)—Fiction.] I. Title.
PZ7.C76955Ye 2014 [Fic]—dc23 2013035459

To Bailey, you were an amazing dog.

ACKNOWLEDGMENTS

Writing a book is a solo event; publishing a book is a team sport. I have a great team to work with, including you as the reader. Without you to read the book, I'm just a person sitting around making stuff up and talking to myself. No one wants to be that person, so thank you.

I have to thank Anica Rissi for believing in this book when it was just an idea, and Liesa Abrams for making sure it went from idea to completed manuscript. The entire crew at Simon Pulse is fantastic to work with, so thanks also go to Michael Strother (my cupcake partner in crime), Bethany Buck, Anna McKean, Amy Jacobson, Karina Granda, and Annette Pollert (and her dad).

My agent, Rachel Coyne, has been with me since the beginning. Thanks for the million things that you do, including laughing at my jokes.

To teachers and librarians who share their love of reading with others, in particular Jennifer Ochoa. Your passion for books inspires me.

I will always owe my parents for getting me addicted to books and my family for putting up with me. After writing this book, my cousin and her husband adopted, and I was blown away by the power of adoption to build new families. If you have any questions, or interest in adoption, please check out www.adoptionsupport.org.

This book is in part about friendship, and I am fortunate to have the most amazing friends. Special thanks to Jamie Hillegonds, Serena Robar, Joelle Anthony, Terra McVoy, Alison Pritchard, Shanna Mahin, Avita Sharma, Wendy Swan, Joanne Levy, Carol Mason, Robyn Harding, and Denise Jaden. To my best friend all through junior high and high school, Laura Sullivan: It's amazing you know me this well and still put up with me.

And to my very best friend, my husband, Bob. I can't imagine this adventure without you.

year of
mistaken
discoveries

chapter one

It was clear that beer didn't make my boyfriend a deep thinker. "I never thought about it before, but Jesus was adopted." Colton nodded slowly, as if realizing something very profound. Or he didn't want to move too quickly in case he got the spins. "Joseph was, like, his stepdad."

I tried to push down my sense of annoyance. He'd promised he wouldn't get drunk tonight, and he'd already moved past drunk and into wasted territory. Then there was the fact that just about everything Colton did lately annoyed me. "What's your point?"

I could see the wheels in Colton's brain trying to churn their way through the waves of Budweiser and come up with a clear thought. "I'm pointing out you've got something in common with Jesus."

"That is so cool," Colton's friend Ryan said. "It's like that six degrees of separation thing."

I managed to avoid rolling my eyes at the both of them. The party at Ryan's was lame, and the revelation I had an inside connection with the Son of God wasn't making it better. We were playing a game, two truths and a lie. You were supposed to say three things about yourself and make one of them a lie. The other person had to guess which one was made up. If they guessed correctly, you had to drink. If you fooled them, they had to drink. When it had been my turn, I'd listed:

—*I'm in love with Colton.*

—*I'm adopted.*

—*I've already met my future roommate at Duke.*

"I can't believe you're adopted," Ryan said again. This was at least the third time he'd said it since I told him he guessed wrong. "How come you never told me before?"

My friend Lydia shoved him in the side. "Maybe Avery didn't tell you because it's none of your business, Mr. McNosy. Drop it, already." She shot a smile over to me. She had picked up on how uncomfortable the whole conversation was making me. Lydia was one of those people who always tried to make things better for other people. She was like the Mother Teresa of our high school. Assuming Mother Teresa was a cheerleader and capable of tossing back Jägermeister shots.

There was no big reason I hadn't told Ryan I was adopted before now. It wasn't a deep dark secret that I didn't want people to know; after all, I'd been the one to make it a part of the game. To be honest, I couldn't always remember who knew and who didn't. Now I wished I hadn't brought it up at all. I'd assumed he would know that the lie was about Duke. Although I was obsessed with getting into Duke, I hadn't even been accepted yet, let alone assigned a roommate.

"We should get going," I said to Colton. I didn't say anything about how earlier he had begged me for a ride so that he wouldn't be out too late since he had practice the next day. "Or you can stay; it's up to you."

Colton sighed as if the weight of the world was pressing down on him. "Why do your parents treat you like you're ten? We're seniors. You're the only person who has to be home by midnight on a Saturday."

Proof of why my parents didn't want me out late came bursting into the room. A group of guys from the football team ran through the living room, carrying on their shoulders some poor junior who was laughing hysterically. They went through the French doors that led outside and tossed the junior into the deep end of the pool. A cheer went up from the crowd. Someone had already dumped hundreds of packets of Crystal Light into the water, dying it a faint orange in honor of our school colors. Go Tiger Cats. Now that we were seniors and creeping closer to graduation, we were starting to get nostalgic for the place we all kept saying we couldn't wait to leave behind. When Ryan's parents got back from Hawaii, he was going to be grounded for life.

"Can't you text them and tell them you're going to be late?" Colton suggested. "Just like a half hour. We're having fun."

I felt like pointing out that we weren't having fun. He was. If I was really honest, I'd given two lies and only one truth. I wasn't in love with Colton. What we had felt like a business arrangement. He was on the football team. I was a cheerleader. We were both popular. Our friends were going out with each other. It was like we were destined to date, regardless of the fact that we had almost nothing in common. When he asked me out last year, my two best friends had been so excited that I got excited too. There was no reason not to love Colton. He was good-looking and, despite the way he was acting at the moment, he was smart. He'd early applied to Harvard and was practically guaranteed a place. It wasn't that I didn't like him; the problem was it didn't go beyond that. I couldn't even say I needed him to grow on me; we'd gone out for almost a year. I could tell the feeling was mutual. Colton liked me, but he didn't love me either. We stayed together because there wasn't really a reason to break up.

"Let's play a different game," my friend Shannon suggested. "We pick a person, and then we each write down two things that describe them on a piece of paper and put it into a bowl. The person has to draw from the bowl and guess who would describe them that way." Shannon got up from the floor, swayed for a moment, and then made it over to the hutch and grabbed the pad of paper by the phone. She started tearing off sheets and passing them around to the crowd that was in the living room. "Okay, we'll start with Avery!"

"No, that's okay," I protested, but I was drowned out. Everyone scribbled something on their sheets and passed them to Shannon, who dumped them into a fancy crystal bowl that was on the shelf. I really hoped she didn't drop it. It looked expensive.

"Okay, close your eyes and pick."

I reached into the bowl and grabbed a slip of paper, reading it out loud for the group. "'Super friendly and best gymnast on the cheer squad.'" I looked around the room. I spotted Liz near the back. She had pink lipstick on her teeth. Liz was a sophomore and an alternate on our cheer squad. She was nice, but she tried entirely too hard. You could smell the desperation to be liked coming off of her in waves. "I'm going to say Liz wrote this," I said.

She squealed. "Oh my God! How'd you guess?" She glanced at the people around her. "I should have put down that she was smart, too, but I could only pick two things."

I smiled. Figuring out it was her hadn't exactly required the deduction skills of Sherlock Holmes. It didn't hurt that she dotted her *i*'s with a heart. She had the handwriting of a sixth grader.

"Must be nice to have a girlfriend who's a gymnast," Ryan said to Colton with a wag of his eyebrows.

"Gotta love a girl who's flexible," Colton shot back, and the two of them clinked beer bottles.

I shot daggers at Colton.

"Keep the game going. Pick another paper," Lydia called out, guessing that I was getting annoyed.

I grabbed another sheet. "'She walks in beauty, like the night . . . and all that's best of dark and bright,'" I read out. My forehead wrinkled. I wasn't even sure what that meant. I looked around the room, but everyone else was looking at each other, trying to figure out who had written it. The words were in tight, all capital letters; it looked like it could have been typed. "I don't know," I said.

"Okay, fess up. Who said it?" Shannon slurred. She pouted when no one volunteered. "C'mon, the point of the game is to figure out who said what."

I felt my cheeks burning. Suddenly I felt embarrassed, like I was the one who had said something private.

"Someone's got a crush on you," Lydia said in a singsong voice.

"Well, I'm not sharing." Colton slapped me on the thigh.

I felt another layer of enamel grind down under my teeth. "I don't want to play anymore." I got up from the sofa and stormed off toward the kitchen, weaving my way through the crowd.

"Dude, you are in trouble," I heard Ryan say as I walked out of the room.

The kitchen was cooler, no doubt due to the fact that someone had left the sliding door to the backyard wide open. A pile of leaves had blown in. Ryan was going to have to rake the kitchen in the morning. I poured myself a glass of water.

"Hey. Are you okay?"

I turned around and saw Brody Garret standing there. He'd transferred to our school at the end of last year, but he never bothered trying to fit in. He wasn't a part of any of the groups at school. He wasn't a jock or a nerd; he didn't play in the band or go out for drama. He wasn't a stoner or on the student council. He wasn't popular, but he wasn't unpopular, either. He always struck me as someone who was studying the rest of us for some kind of in-depth story on the modern high school. He had this way of staring at you that made you feel as if he was really seeing you. Seeing what no one else noticed.

"I'm fine."

"Do you need a ride home?" He motioned to the door. "I can give you one if you want. I don't mind leaving."

I stared at him. Brody was slim, but fit. He had the body of a dancer; he moved like he had no joints, almost like he floated. His smile was crooked, with one side of his mouth pulling up higher than the other. He looked to me like he belonged in New York, not the middle of Michigan. He stood out in our school. I cocked my head to the side. He might have been different enough to write down that odd description of me. I wanted to ask him, but I didn't know if he meant it as a compliment, or a way to make fun of me.

"Aren't you enjoying the party?" I asked.

Brody looked around the room. Shannon ran through the kitchen squealing until one of the football players grabbed her and tossed her over his shoulder. She was beating on his back, laughing while he carried her into the living room. There was a splash and a loud cheer outside; it sounded like someone had either jumped into the pool or maybe tossed in one of the lounge chairs. Brody glanced over at me and raised an eyebrow.

"This is supposed to be the party of the year," I told him.

"It's only October. I'm holding out for better."

The sound of someone vomiting in the powder room next door carried through the wall. "Sort of hard to top this," I said.

"Dare to dream." He smiled and I found myself smiling back.

Colton burst into the kitchen with Ryan and Karl, Lydia's boyfriend. Brody took a step to the side. I hadn't realized we were standing that close. Colton fell on his knees in front of me. "You gotta forgive me." He turned around and motioned to his friends, who also went down on their knees, although Ryan almost fell over completely. "They want you to forgive me too."

"Colton," I said. "Get up."

He shuffled forward on his knees. "Not until you forgive

me. I was being a pig." Ryan started oinking loudly behind Colton. Karl tried to oink, but it came out more like a snort.

"I don't really want to talk about this here," I said, my voice low. I didn't want to look up to see Brody's expression.

"No problem." Colton leaped up. "Gentlemen, if you'll excuse us." His arm circled around me and he pulled me into the pantry. He shut the door behind us. He pressed me up against the shelves. The smells of cinnamon, basil, and pepper filled my nose from the spice rack behind me. "I was just joking around. I didn't mean to piss you off," he said.

Colton started to kiss my neck, his hands running along my side. This was another problem I had with Colton. Every time we were alone, it was like playing Whac-A-Mole with his hands. This wasn't helped by the fact we didn't have much to talk about with each other so making out seemed like the only thing to do. Colton did this thing where he would rub his thumb over my nipple rapidly as if he were using a video game controller. I think he thought it was supposed to be sexually exciting. Instead it felt like he was trying to start a fire Boy Scout style. I pushed his hand down.

It wasn't that I was against sex, or that I was against the idea of sex with Colton in particular (although the nipple-chafing thing didn't bode well). My official answer was I was waiting for it to be the right time. The truth was I wasn't sure if there was a right time or place. I knew my birth mom had gotten pregnant in high school. She was only sixteen when I was born. What the adoption information forms didn't say was if my mom had tried to take precautions. Had she and my dad used a condom? What if she was hyperfertile and that was a trait I'd inherited? For all I knew, my eggs were six times the normal size, making the odds of any sperm missing them nearly nil. Or maybe my birth mom didn't worry about birth control. Maybe she slept with everyone. What if I was genetically predisposed to being a slut? It was possible I would sleep with Colton and discover I was sex obsessed and wanton. I might not be able to stop. I might start having sex with everyone I met.

Then there was the fact I knew I didn't love Colton. And I certainly didn't love how he let all of his friends think that we were going at it all the time. If I was going to finally go all the way, it wasn't going to be in Ryan Lee's pantry with Colton smelling like cheap beer. I sighed.

Colton stopped kissing my neck and backed up a step. "Sorry if I'm bothering you." His voice was annoyed.

"I don't want to do this."

He ran his hand through his hair, leaving it sticking up in the back. "You know what, me neither."

I was about to roll my eyes when I realized he wasn't talking about making out. "You're breaking up with me?"

Colton sighed. "At least try and sound upset about it."

chapter two

Time seemed to freeze. Colton stood against the pantry shelves, boxes of cereal lined up behind him. It was like he'd brought his posse of the Lucky Charms leprechaun, Tony the Tiger, and the Rice Krispies boys to stick up for him.

"You seriously want to break up?" I asked.

Colton sighed. "Maybe." We stood in the pantry a few inches apart, staring at each other. "All we do is fight."

I wanted to argue with him, but the irony of fighting about if we fight too much wasn't lost on me. Half of me wanted to jump at what Colton was suggesting and end it, and the other half of me was freaking out and wanting to grab ahold of him before he could leave. I felt myself starting to tear up. It wasn't that I was sad. It was that I was frustrated. How could I not know what I wanted?

"Hey, don't cry." Colton shifted nervously. He looked around and grabbed a roll of paper towels and passed them over to me.

I wanted to throw the paper towels or scream, but if tears were making him uncomfortable, me losing it would really make him flee. "We've been together a long time," I said.

"Yeah."

"Do you want to date someone else?" I asked.

His eyes shifted away from mine. "No." I would bet money he was lying, but I wasn't sure if it was to me or to himself. Colton liked to think of himself as one of the good guys, and he was. I'd never worried about him cheating on me.

My throat felt tight, like I couldn't squeeze out any more words. I was like a prisoner waiting for a judge to pass sentence. Now I wanted it over. If he was going to dump me, I wanted him to do it and get it over with. This felt like waiting for the doctor to give you a shot; you know it's coming, you know it's going to hurt, but the waiting is the worst. The horrid part is that I wanted him to do it.

"Jeez, I'm wasted. Do we have to do the serious stuff now?" Colton rubbed his forehead. "Maybe we could just take a break," Colton finally said. "Talk about it some other time."

"A break?" What did that even mean? We were going to put our relationship on hold?

"You know, take some time. Sort out what we want to do. Sometime when we're both sober." I could see the idea growing on him. It sounded really reasonable and didn't make any real decision. No wonder Colton was the president of our class. He was born to be a politician.

"Okay, sure. We'll take a break." It seemed easier to agree since I didn't know what I wanted either.

Colton let out a low breath; he was relieved. "You'll be okay?"

"Me?" I squeaked. I wiped my eyes with a wad of paper towels. What would make him think I wasn't okay? Just because I was standing in a pantry crying? I shrugged. "I'm fine."

Colton was already stepping out of the pantry, making his escape. "We'll talk in a couple days, okay?"

I smiled and nodded like I couldn't imagine anything I'd rather do. He squeezed my hand and then ducked out. I shut the door behind him and slid down so I was sitting on the floor. I stared at the giant bag of organic dog kibble across from me. I wondered how long it would take the news to spread at the party. I didn't want to ever leave the pantry. Heck, I might not need to. There was plenty of food in here, a couple of cases of Diet Coke on the floor, and even a bucket. I'd become a pantry hermit. I'd come out only in the middle of the night when the rest of the world was sleeping to take a shower and then come right back to live on stale Froot Loops and dried beans. I wondered how Ryan's parents would feel about me moving in here. If I offered to do a few chores around the place, they might let me stay.

I let myself sit there for a few more minutes. I needed to find Shannon and Lydia and tell them what happened. This was the kind of situation that called for good friends. Maybe an ice-cream binge. Maybe they could both come over and stay the night. I licked my finger and ran it under my eyes to make sure I didn't have a huge mascara smear and fluffed my hair.

I flung open the pantry door. There was a group of band girls standing by the sink. They went instantly still when they saw me, like animals under the glare of a predator. I stared at them, waiting to see if they would say anything, but they suddenly acted fascinated by pouring the bag of Doritos they had into a bowl.

I peeked casually around the corner into the living room. There was still a group of people playing some kind of game, but I didn't see either Lydia or Shannon. I could hear Colton's voice outside, so I slid past the patio door and went looking through the rest of the house. The dining room table was surrounded by people playing quarters, but no sign of my friends. I knew they wouldn't have left. One, they both had later curfews than me, and two, I could still see Karl's car parked right outside in the driveway. There were a few people slipping upstairs, but most of those were couples looking for an empty bedroom.

I heard a roar coming from the basement. There was a media room down there, and it sounded like they were playing some kind of video game. Most likely shooting zombies. What could be more fun on a Friday night than blowing away the undead? I slipped through the crowd, heading toward the stairs, smiling vaguely at people I knew but not stopping so that I wouldn't get sucked into a conversation.

"Avery!"

I froze in place. I knew that voice. I turned around. It was Nora. She was standing next to Brody.

"Look who showed up—the Grim Reaper," said a voice next to me with a snicker.

Nora was waving across the room at me like we were still best friends. I wanted to drop to the floor and crawl away, but it was too late. There wasn't a moment when I decided I didn't want to be friends with Nora anymore. It happened by degrees. At some point the only thing we had in common was the fact that we used to be friends, and that had a tendency to make things awkward.

Nora was already weaving her way through the crowd. I could see a few people looking over, surprised to see her. Nora wasn't the type to typically show up at a house party. She wasn't picked on or bullied at school, but she didn't really fit in, either. Not that Nora tried to fit in. If anything, she seemed to go out of her way to be as different as possible from everyone else. She tended to wear head-to-toe black, and last year she'd gotten an eyebrow ring. She sent out a vibe that practically screamed, *Back off*. It was hard for me to believe there'd been a time when we'd been inseparable.

When I met Nora in first grade, I desperately wanted to be

best friends with her, partly because she said she was going to be a mermaid when she grew up, but mostly because she was also adopted.

Our teacher, Ms. Klee, had told us to draw a picture of what we wanted to be when we became adults. The class bent over their papers and turned out drawings of police officers, race-car drivers, doctors, football players, and even one president complete with a billowing flag in the background. I sat there, sniffing the end of my Pacific Blue crayon, hoping that the waxy smell would inspire me. I had no idea what I wanted to be. I shifted in my seat, the sound of everyone else hard at work making me anxious. I finally started a picture of a teacher, not because I had an interest in teaching, but because I thought it might make Ms. Klee happy.

"Pssst. Can I borrow your silver?" Nora's fingers pinched the top of the crayon lined up with the others like a church choir in my box.

They were new crayons. My mom had gotten me the giant sixty-four colors box, complete with built-in sharpener, but it seemed stingy not to share. I nodded and Nora pulled the crayon out and went back to work. Ms. Klee stopped between our desks, smiling as she glanced at my page. Her eyebrow went up when she looked down at Nora's.

"It's a mermaid," Nora explained, outlining the scales on the tail with my crayon.

"It's a very pretty mermaid," Ms. Klee acknowledged.

"But you know you can't be one when you grow up. They're make-believe."

Nora didn't even look up from her picture, but I could see her fingers gripping the crayon tighter.

"My mom says we can be whatever we want, as long as we're willing to work for it," I said, sitting up straight. Nora shot me a look of gratitude. Ms. Klee moved down the aisle without another word, not willing to enter into an argument with a six-year-old on the viability of her career prospects.

At lunch Nora plunked down next to me, pulling items out of her bag. She had egg-salad sandwiches sprinkled with bright fuchsia pickled beets. My sliced turkey with Swiss cheese looked practically gray in comparison.

"Do you really want to be a mermaid when you grow up?" I asked.

Nora shrugged. "Maybe. I like to swim. I might miss having legs, though. And you can't have a TV underwater. Not having a TV would get boring, I think."

I nodded. You couldn't argue with logic like that.

"Do you really want to be a teacher?" she asked.

"Not really. I don't know what I want to do."

Nora's lips were tinted pink from the beets. "My mom's a mermaid; that's why I put it down."

I looked at her out the side of my eyes, trying to figure out if she was teasing me.

"Well, my real mom *might* be a mermaid," Nora admitted.

"I don't really know anything about her. I'm adopted."

The bite of sandwich I had in my mouth fell onto my wax paper with a wet plop. I almost couldn't believe the coincidence. "I'm adopted too."

Nora reached over and stole one of my grapes. "Well then, your birth mom could have been a mermaid too. You never know. Those things can happen."

chapter three

Before Nora could reach me, Shannon grabbed my arm.

"Holy shit. Did you and Colton really break up?" Shannon whispered. Lydia was standing right behind her, looking ready to cry.

"Not officially. We're taking a break."

Shannon's right eyebrow went up. "A break?" At least I wasn't the only one who thought the whole "break" concept was weird.

"Hey," Nora said, reaching my side. At least Brody hadn't followed her.

I shot Shannon and Lydia a look letting them know I had no intention of getting into the Colton discussion with Nora right there.

My friends aren't a group of mean girls. Everyone always

tries to make cheerleaders into the villains, like they pass out uniforms and attitude at the same time. People see a group of girls in cheerleader uniforms and assume we must all be class A bitches, but we're not. It's not like there is some official kind of ranking, but I guess we're three of the most popular girls at school. You can tell there are expectations of those who have that kind of social ranking, and one of them is that popular girls don't hang out with someone like Nora. Her dark, brooding "I'm so very misunderstood" shtick didn't blend with many people. They found her to be a downer. Then there was the fact she was always telling wild stories. Half the time I couldn't even tell if she believed the stuff she was saying, or if she was making them weirder and weirder just to see how people would respond.

"Hey." I pressed my mouth into what I hoped would pass as a smile. "I didn't expect to see you here. I didn't know you and Ryan were friends."

Nora looked around as if she almost found herself surprised to be at the party. "Yeah. Not so much."

Shannon held out a can to me. "Hey, Avery, I got you a Diet Coke for the road." Her eyes slid over to Nora. She took in her outfit, which made Nora look like a crow. Shannon was Nora's exact opposite. She never met a shade of pink that she didn't love. It was like being friends with someone made of cotton candy. She smiled at Nora. "There's a bunch of stuff to drink in the kitchen. I don't know what you like, but I'm sure Ryan has it."

"Blood of virgins, mostly," Nora said in a flat voice. "Look at the bright side—you probably don't need to worry."

Neither Shannon nor Lydia laughed. I poked Nora in the side with my elbow. "She's joking," I clarified. I felt my blood pressure rise. It was just like Nora; she didn't even try to be normal. Would it kill her to make an effort to get along with my friends? I hadn't talked to her in months and she had to pick tonight to show up, just when I thought things couldn't get worse.

"I need to get going. I'm late for my curfew," I said, as if I was really bummed I had to cut this conversation short. This is where normal people would say how they were glad to see you and hoped you had a good night, but Nora just stood there. "These guys are coming over," I explained. Shannon and Lydia nodded in tandem.

"I need to talk to you," Nora said.

"It's not a great time." This was the understatement of the year. "Maybe give me a call tomorrow or something," I suggested. All I wanted to do was get out of this party, and it was turning into one of those horror movies where the person's feet are stuck, or sinking into the floor.

"I came here to find you," Nora said. "It's important."

Shannon and Lydia stood behind me, ready to help me make my escape. I couldn't think of a single thing that Nora and I had to talk about at that instant. I opened my mouth to tell her that she'd have to call me.

"Come on, you can't spare five minutes? For old times' sake?" Nora pleaded.

"Fine. Look, can you guys meet me by my car in five?" I turned back to Nora. "It can only be a few minutes. I'm late for curfew."

"I'll tell Karl I'm leaving," Lydia said.

Shannon shot Nora a dirty look. "Sure. I'll grab my stuff and text my parents to let them know I'm staying at your place. We'll be out in five." She stressed the five.

As soon as I stepped outside, the air hit me like a sharp slap. It was at least twenty degrees colder outside than in the house. A layer of frost had covered everything since the party started, making the windows of the cars parked all over the lawn opaque. The grass under our feet was crunchy, like walking on corn chips. My breath plumed out like a dragon's.

"So, what's up?" I asked.

Nora looked down the street. "You decide on a senior project yet?"

Of all the things I thought Nora might have hunted me down about, homework wasn't even on the list. Northside High made every senior do a project and present it as a requirement for graduation. We were supposed to partner up with someone so that we could learn teamwork. Did she actually think we'd do a project together after all this time?

"Uh. Yeah. Colton and I are doing a project on education reform." As soon as the words were out of my mouth, I paused.

Would we still be doing the project? We'd come up with the idea over the summer. We'd already been working on it since the first week in September. Colton planned to major in public policy when he got to Harvard. I didn't know what I wanted to major in, but I was sure our project was going to be the perfect thing that would put my Duke application over the top. I'd already turned in my early application and mentioned it. What was I going to do if we broke up? My stomach tightened. Getting into Duke was everything.

"Wow. Sounds riveting," Nora said.

I felt a flash of annoyance. "It's an important issue."

Nora nodded. "I bet." Her voice came out flat. "I just thought you'd do something you felt passionate about. Like writing a book or doing a book drive for kids or something."

I snorted. "Can you imagine Colton wanting to write a book?"

"No. I can imagine you doing it." She met my eyes. "You used to be a great writer. Remember those stories you used to write down all the time?"

"I had an overactive imagination." I felt suddenly embarrassed, like she'd dragged out photos from junior high where I'd shot up really tall and looked as awkward as I felt. It wasn't that I thought there was anything wrong with writing, but it felt sort of artsy-fartsy. I couldn't imagine the Duke admissions team being impressed with my bad poetry. "The stories were stupid."

Nora was quiet for a beat. "I thought they were great."

Now I felt like I had somehow insulted her, which made no sense, because they were my stories. "Anyway, if you're still looking for a partner, I could check around and see if I know anyone looking." For the life of me I couldn't imagine any of my friends wanting to partner with Nora.

"I'm partnered with Brody," Nora said.

Her answer struck me like an electric shock. "Oh. I didn't know you guys were friends." There was no reason for me to feel surprised. It wasn't like she owed me a list of who she hung out with. It wasn't that unusual, they were both part of the Island of Misfit Toys, the people who didn't really fit into any other social crowd. "He seems like a nice guy."

"Nice?" Nora shot me a look. "He's not a golden retriever." She pulled her sweatshirt sleeves down so they were covering her hands. "Brody's cool."

"What are you guys doing for a project? Something with photography?" I glanced back at Ryan's house to see if Shannon and Lydia were coming.

"I quit the photography store."

I spun around, surprised. "When?" Nora had worked at the camera store at the mall since our sophomore year. Her dad had been really into photography, and when he still lived with them, he'd had a darkroom in their basement for developing film. He'd left a year ago, trading Nora and her mom in for his secretary, who was still in her twenties. It was gross. Nora had grown up knowing about telephoto lenses and what someone meant by the term "f-stop." I knew she was mad at her dad for leaving, but I hadn't thought she'd give up taking pictures. I couldn't imagine her without a camera.

"A month ago. I didn't see the point." She shrugged. "Our project was to find my birth mom." She saw my expression. "I know. A waste of time, right? Isn't that what you're always saying?" Nora had been abandoned at a Catholic hospital in Costa Rica when she was a few weeks old. The pointlessness of searching for her parents when there wasn't any information on them didn't stop Nora from lurking on various adoptee websites and blogs. Nora had always maintained that I couldn't understand how she felt because I knew so much more than she did. While my parents never tried to act like my adoption was a secret, or something to be ashamed of, I couldn't shake the feeling that they wished it were something we could pretend hadn't really happened.

My parents always told me they were there to talk about how I felt about being adopted, but their tone told me they didn't really want to discuss it. It was the same as when they gave me the big sex talk. They told me I could ask anything then, too, but you could tell they really hoped I wasn't going to ask them anything too awkward or embarrassing, like asking about what people meant by the term "blow job." Saying you're willing to talk about anything is the kind of thing you're supposed to say if you're a parent.

"It's not that I think it's a waste," I hedged. I really hoped she didn't want me to somehow help with her project. The fact that we were both adopted didn't seem reason enough to me. I shivered from the cold. "It'll be hard to find her."

"She contacted me."

My mouth fell open. "What?"

Nora chuckled. "You should see your face. Yep. I was on one of those online adoption sites and she reached out to me. Her name is Carla. She told me she never abandoned me."

"So a bunch of Catholic nuns stole you?" The disbelief in my voice came through loud and clear.

"No." Her tone took on a note of condescension, like she was talking to a small child who was learning disabled. "Carla told me that there are people down there who take babies because foreign adoptive parents will pay big bucks. You know what my parents paid for my adoption, right? You think money like that in a poor country doesn't inspire people to do shit they shouldn't? Carla was told that this guy was going to take me to a medical clinic for vaccinations. She didn't know what had happened to me until after I'd already been adopted."

My bullshit meter was going off. The whole scenario seemed over the top. Nora was watching for my reaction, so I tried to keep my expression neutral. It wouldn't be the first time she'd tried to get a rise out of me. "Listen, you don't have to come up with some kind of story to get my attention."

"It's not my story. It's hers." She barked out a bitter laugh.

"You knew it was a lie right off the bat. I'm always teasing you about being the Mary Poppins type, but you see through her and I didn't see a thing." Her voice was hard and cold. She didn't meet my eyes. My stomach sank. This wasn't one of Nora's elaborate lies. There was something more going on.

chapter four

I tried to make sense of what Nora was saying. The conversation was moving too fast. There were bursts of music and voices from the party whenever the door opened that made it hard to focus. "She wasn't your mom? She made it up?" I asked.

"The whole thing was a scam. She asked me for money. She'd pay me back as soon as possible, of course, and then we could meet face-to-face and have a great mother-daughter reunion. Blah, blah, blah." She smiled, but it didn't extend to her eyes. "Even as much as I wanted to believe she was my mom, I knew then it was a con. I might be stupid, but I'm not a total moron."

My stomach sank. "You're not stupid. What she did was twisted. She should be arrested, or sued, or something. Did you tell the cops?"

"Why? So it could be public how pathetic I am? Poor sad

orphan searching for her mommy." She tried to make it sound sarcastic, but the pain was on her face. A tear ran down her cheek.

It took a lot to hurt Nora. When we were in junior high, some of the high school kids made fun of her on the bus for what she was wearing. She turned around, stared them in the eye, and told them she didn't give a shit about their opinion, so they should feel free to stop giving it. Nora was tough, but she was crying now.

"I'm sorry," I said. I reached for her, but she backed up a step, slipping a bit on the icy ground. I had the sense she was afraid if I touched her she'd fly apart.

"It doesn't matter." She shrugged, her chin jutting up in the air.

"Okay, time to hit the road!" Shannon called out from the front door. She had her giant hot-pink Coach bag thrown over one shoulder and a hat jammed over her hair. Lydia planted a kiss on Karl and then pushed him back inside toward the party. I waved at them, holding up a finger so they would give us a minute more.

"Listen, why don't you come over tomorrow?" I acted like it was no big deal, even though I couldn't remember the last time I'd invited her to my house. "We could just hang out if you want. We haven't caught up in forever."

For a second I thought she was going to start crying again, but she swallowed hard and then put a smile on her face. "No, it's okay. I only came by to give you something." She reached into her beaten leather messenger bag and pulled out one of those black Moleskine notebooks. Written on the front in silver pen was: *Field Guide to Finding Your Family*. She passed it over to me. I flipped it open and recognized her tiny slanted writing. "It's everything I learned looking for my mom. Thought you might find it useful if you ever went looking for yours," she explained.

I stared down at the notebook. As kids we'd made a blood vow (not much blood, to be technical; we'd each poked our thumbs with a tack, but it hurt like a son of a bitch) that we'd help each other to find our birth moms, even if the search took us to the ends of the earth. I couldn't speak for Nora, but I'd been pretty sure at some point we'd be crashing through the Costa Rican jungle in full-on Indiana Jones outfits, hot on the trail of her mom. Somewhere around junior high I'd lost interest in the quest, but she never had.

"I can't take this," I said, trying to pass the worn notebook back to her. "I'm not looking for my birth mom."

"I want you to have it." She shrugged. "Besides, you never know."

"What about you? Don't you need it?"

"Nah. I'm done." Her mouth was pressed into a thin line.

I'd bugged Nora for years to give up on finding her mom, but now that she had, I wanted to convince her to keep looking.

"You ready to go?" Shannon said, walking up. "I can hear the ice cream in your freezer calling to me."

"Well, there you go. You don't want to ignore that. Once Ben and Jerry start speaking to you, it's the end of the night," Nora said. She backed away with a wave.

"Calling front seat!" Lydia yelled out. She ran over to my car in her impossibly high heels. Shannon was trying to argue with her, but only halfheartedly.

"Hey, Avery?" Nora had stopped. She seemed to be debating something, but then stepped forward and gave me a hug. I froze in place. It was safe to say Nora was not the kind of person you'd describe as a hugger. "Thanks," she mumbled.

"For what?" I asked.

"For everything." She winked. "SOC forever."

I'd almost forgotten our shorthand. SOC stood for Sister of Choice. In second grade Nora got the idea that since we were both adopted, maybe we were sisters. We practically had proof: We loved vanilla more than chocolate, couldn't stand the smell of cauliflower cooking, and could touch our tongues to the tips of our noses. We'd gotten really excited about the idea, until my mom sat us down and explained that it was unlikely we were twins separated at birth, not the least because Nora was part Costa Rican and I was clearly as white as they come, and having a secret twin was apparently the kind of thing the adoption agency would have mentioned in the official paperwork. When we got back to my room, I'd burst into tears. I had been so sure we were sisters. Nora patted my back and told me not to be sad, we were better than sisters, and after all, being born sisters was just an accident of birth. We were sisters of choice. SOC. Whenever we would leave each other we would call out "SOC," and we signed it at the bottom of all our notes to each other.

"I remember," I said, but she'd already turned away. In her black clothing she disappeared into the inky darkness just a few steps away from the house.

"Freezing in here!" Shannon called out, startling me. "We need some heat!"

I jumped into the car and turned it over, the heater cranking on with a loud whoosh, blowing ice-cold air over us. The skin on my arms puckered up in goose bumps. I shoved Nora's notebook into my purse. Lydia started fooling around with the car radio, turning it up when she heard a song she liked. I should have offered to give Nora a ride home—we didn't even live that far from each other—but she was already gone.

"So what was that all about?" Shannon asked.

"I don't know," I admitted.

"Let's get down to the important stuff. So start talking. What's up with you and Colton?" Shannon leaned forward so she was practically in the front seat with Lydia and me. "What the hell does taking a break even mean?"

That's all it took for me to forget Nora. I launched into a blow-by-blow breakdown of our pantry discussion, and how I wasn't even sure what I wanted anymore. I didn't think about Nora again.

chapter five

They say bad things happen in threes. That should have warned me that there were still two to go.

Saturday morning my mom tapped on my bedroom door a few minutes past eight. Considering the three of us had stayed up until after four talking about Colton and the definition of a break, no one was very thrilled.

Shannon rolled over on the floor in my sleeping bag, pulling a pillow over her head. "You have got to be kidding me."

"I'm never drinking again," Lydia mumbled. "It tastes like I slept with a dirty sock in my mouth."

"That's probably because you were kissing Karl," Shannon said. Lydia tossed her pillow at her.

My mom tapped on the door again, this time a bit louder, and poked her head in.

"You girls still snoozing?" she asked in a loud whisper.

I rolled my eyes at Shannon. What did it look like we were doing? Both of my parents were morning people. This was one of the sure signs I was adopted. If left alone, I could easily sleep past ten. My parents both got up before six a.m. without using an alarm. Even on the weekends. They talked about how great it was to get a jump start on the day. There was not a single atom in my body that felt like jump-starting anything before lunch.

"We stayed up late talking," I explained. "We don't want breakfast or anything." My dad liked to make huge breakfasts on the weekend. During the week he worked as a software engineer, but on the weekends he channeled his inner Food Network chef. He even insisted on wearing this totally dorky apron that had I KISS EVEN BETTER THAN I COOK on the front. I knew Lydia was in no shape to face breakfast, and Shannon, while she wasn't a food Nazi or anything, had been a bit chubby in junior high and now could tell you the calorie content of any food item. When she saw the amount of butter my dad put in everything, she would stroke out.

"I suspect everyone's got a lot planned for their weekend," Mom said.

The whole point of a weekend was to not have anything planned. This concept escaped my mom. She worked as a lawyer for a women's rights association, and she wasn't happy unless she was juggling at least seventy things. Overachiever didn't even begin to describe her. Last year, in one day she testified before the state senate on the importance of contraception rights, came home and baked a hundred cupcakes for our cheer camp bake sale, and fixed the dishwasher, which had broken the night before. My mom had this way of making me tired just watching her.

"We might head over to the mall later," I said. Lydia nodded, but Shannon still had the pillow over her face.

Mom's brow wrinkled up. Most likely she was disappointed we weren't planning on doing a door-to-door awareness campaign against female genital mutilation. "We need to do some stuff as a family today," she said. "I'm afraid you girls will have to go out to the mall another day."

I rolled over and looked at her. There hadn't been any family activities listed on the giant calendar that hung in the kitchen, and we were the kind of family that lived and died by the schedule.

"We need to have a family discussion." Mom was smiling, but I could tell she was serious about something.

"Oh."

Lydia raised an eyebrow at me, but I had no idea what my mom was talking about. My stomach rolled over. Something was up.

"Do you girls need a ride home?"

Lydia sat up in bed. It was clear this party was over. "No, I can give my mom a call to pick us up. We can drop Shannon off on the way home."

As soon as the door shut, Lydia turned to me. "Does she know about the party last night?"

Shannon yanked the pillow off her face. Her hair was sticking up. "Shit. Did someone call everyone's parents and tell them there was booze? My folks will kill me." Shannon had gotten caught drinking at her cousin's wedding in June. The guy working the bar thought she was hot and kept slipping her cranberry and vodka. She'd been on house arrest for a month. The last thing she needed was to be grounded all over again.

"I have no idea," I said, yanking off the covers.

As soon as Shannon and Lydia had pulled out of the driveway, my parents called me outside to join them in raking leaves. My hair was still damp from the quick shower I'd taken. I hadn't wanted to face them until I had a shower. It's hard to prepare yourself for anything when you still have on yesterday's undies and dirty hair. I picked up a rake and started to pile the red and gold maple leaves for my dad to bag up. I wasn't sure if I should start by confessing and hope that the honesty policy would gain me some valuable karma points, or if I should stick with the Fifth Amendment until I knew exactly what they knew. Having a mom who was a lawyer and a software genius for a dad meant needing to bring my A game to any questioning.

We raked in silence for a while. I wondered if we were going to pretend that there was nothing going on other than a sudden need to clean the yard. "So . . ." I let my voice trail off.

"We need to talk to you about something," my dad started. Both my mom and I were looking at him, but he didn't seem like he knew what to say next.

"You got your letter from Duke yesterday." My mom pulled a thin white envelope out of her jacket pocket. I could just make out the raised Duke University seal. "We shouldn't have opened your mail, but we were excited." Her voice didn't sound remotely excited at this point.

My heart lurched in my chest. I'd early applied to Duke. It's the only place I really wanted to go next year. Both of my parents went there. So did their parents, along with various aunts and uncles. (Minus my uncle Raymond, who was rarely spoken of in the family except with a "bless his heart," which was meant to excuse his vast number of screwups.) I grew up with the Duke Blue Devil logo on everything: beach towels, sweatshirts, coffee mugs, even a set of Christmas ornaments. Last summer we had driven down to the campus, and my parents walked around with me, pointing out their favorite spots. They made sure I knew what place made great pizza, or how to score valuable basketball tickets when the time came. My mom took me over to the Chi Omega house, her sorority. The girls all made a big deal out of her stopping by. Most of them were wearing matching T-shirts with the Greek letters embossed on them. I'd assumed that between being a legacy applicant and my decent grades I'd be able to squeak in for admission. Apparently, upon reflection, Duke could ferret out that while my parents belonged, there was something about me that wasn't quite up to snuff. I wasn't supposed to hear until December. If they'd sent the letter already, it wasn't good news.

"I didn't get in," I said, hoping they would tell me I was wrong. I wanted to kick the pile of leaves I'd made.

My dad let out a breath in a whoosh. He must have been holding it while he waited for me to figure it out. "They didn't turn you down; they deferred your application."

"Deferred? What does that mean?" Why was everything in my life suddenly dropped into this purgatory state of nowheresville? Now Duke wanted to "take a break" too.

Mom fidgeted with her rake. "It's not that bad."

It's my experience that when people have to tell you something isn't that bad, it means it really does suck.

"They're going to hold your application until the general application round," Dad explained. "In some ways you can see it as a positive. This gives you a chance to wow the heck out of them over the next few months." He gave a fist pump like there was no telling what exciting stuff I might do to impress them.

I thought *I* was supposed to be the cheerleader in this family. "But they didn't like me enough to let me in now," I pointed out.

"Admission is more competitive than ever these days," Mom added.

"And we're not surrendering. The Scott family gets back

up when we're knocked down," Dad added in his new, overly cheerful voice. At this rate he was going to become one of those motivational speakers who show up on Dr. Phil and have hair that looks a bit too perfect.

I pressed my mouth together. But I wasn't really a Scott, was I? The truth was Duke had always been competitive. No one had ever picked Duke as his or her safety school. My parents were able to make the cut, and I wasn't. My grades were good, but I had to really work for them. I knew from talking to my grandparents that school had come easy to my parents. I could remember my dad going over my math homework with me and then being surprised that even with his explanation I didn't have a clue how to solve for x.

Mom jumped in. "We set up an appointment for you to talk to a school placement consultant. She can meet with you to go over your options and help you come up with a plan B on the off chance that you need it. She comes very highly recommended."

I had no doubt about this. My parents never did anything halfway. There was a whole shelf of books on parenting in our living room. Our family doctor was rated number one in the city. When they built the house, they'd researched local contractors until they knew who would be the best for the job. They bought into a neighborhood that would have me attend the best school. They didn't buy appliances unless *Consumer Reports* had given them the golden ass-kiss of acceptance. There was nothing in this house that didn't meet their high expectations. Except maybe me.

Dad grabbed a pile of leaves and shoved them into a bag. "I've come up with a bunch of ideas. You can do some extra volunteer work with your mom's agency. We can highlight the stuff you did last year for the drama club. That shows being well-rounded, things like that." He smiled at me before bending down to scoop up more leaves.

Mom leaned forward and hugged me. "It's going to be okay."

I wondered if she was trying to convince me, or herself. "I know," I lied, because I knew that was the answer that she wanted to hear. My nose was starting to run from the cold, and I wiped it on my jacket sleeve.

"Just wait until those admissions counselors get a look at the senior project you've got planned with Colton," Dad said. "That's going to blow their socks off."

My stomach free-fell to the ground. I had no idea if Colton and I were still doing the project together. "Colton and I are kinda taking a break."

I winced when I saw my parents exchange the look. The kind that said, *Poor thing*. I was trying to figure out how to explain I was fine when the phone rang inside the house.

"What do you say we go out for lunch today and plan our strategy?" Dad suggested, while Mom dashed into the house to grab the call. He took the rake from my hand and hung it in the garage. He peeled his coat off and headed into the kitchen, his nose red from the cold.

All I wanted to do was crawl into bed and pull the covers back over my head and pretend the last twenty-four hours hadn't happened. I wasn't sure I was up to acting like I thought everything was going to be fine. And giving my parents a blow by blow of my "break" with Colton over a lunch at Applebee's sounded nauseating. I followed my dad inside. I was trying to come up with an excuse that wouldn't sound like an excuse when I noticed he wasn't talking to me and instead was staring at my mom.

My mom was gripping the phone, and her face was gray. My dad touched her arm lightly, and it seemed to let the air out of her; she sank down on the closest chair. She shook her head at him, waving him off so she could finish the conversation.

"Of course. I appreciate your call." She clicked off the phone and put it down really carefully, as if she thought it was a grenade that might explode.

"Hon?" Dad's voice was almost a whisper.

I could visibly see my mom pulling herself together. That's when I knew bad things happen in threes and the third was about to hit.

"I'm so sorry, sweetheart." Her voice caught. "Nora's dead."

chapter six

I wasn't a kid. I understood the concept that people died. When our cat Mr. Mittens passed away, my parents didn't try and convince me that he'd gone to live on a farm, or had decided to move on to a new family; they told me the truth. But while I understood the concept of death in practical terms, I didn't expect it to happen to someone I knew. The idea that Nora was simply gone seemed impossible. It would have been easier for me to believe that she'd sprouted wings and ridden off on a unicorn. The past three days had slid by in a fog. It was as if the real world was turned up too high. Lights were too bright, sounds too loud, everything seemed to chafe and rub me wrong. I would do something normal like brush my teeth and then think, *Nora's never going to brush her teeth again.* Then I would feel light-headed and have to sit down.

I didn't think there would be anything worse than someone dying, but there was. After my mom had told me Nora was dead, I sat there shocked.

"What happened? Was it a car accident?" I finally asked.

"No, it wasn't a car accident." Her eyes didn't meet mine.

"What happened?"

"It doesn't matter," my mom said. "What's important is that you know that Nora was your friend. Losing her is a tragedy, for you, for her, for her family, for everybody." I could see my dad raise an eyebrow, questioning what she was saying.

I knew something else was wrong. "What happened to her? Did someone kill her?"

My mom looked shocked. "What? No. No one killed her. Why would you think something like that? It was an accident." Mom took my hands and squeezed them. She pulled me slightly so I was facing her and took a deep breath. "Nora died from an overdose."

Dad gasped in shock. It didn't make sense. I'd seen her last night and she hadn't been high or drunk. I would have sworn she was completely sober. There had to be a mistake. "Nora didn't take drugs." My parents were looking at me with sympathetic eyes. I felt slightly panicked that they didn't believe me. "She didn't. I'm sure of it."

"They were pills from home. Her mom was on medications, and it looks like Nora took them." Mom's voice was calm and stable. "It's not clear if she wanted to just . . . mentally escape, or if it was on purpose."

My mind screeched to a stop. "On purpose? People think Nora killed herself?" My stomach clenched, and a wave of hot acid crept up my throat. It felt as if the room was closing in on me.

Dad winced as if I'd slapped him. He glanced at Mom, hoping she would deny it. She took a deep breath as if she were in one of her yoga classes and trying to find her center. "Nora was really troubled. She's struggled on and off with depression for a long time."

I stood up. "No. This isn't happening." Mom tried to hold on to my hand, but I yanked it away. I felt panicked. "I'm sorry." My voice hitched.

She pulled me up. "It's okay, baby." She wrapped her arms around me, and a second later my dad had his arms around both of us. I wanted to cry, but it felt like my insides had been scoured out with a rusty scoop, raw and empty.

Since I'd heard the news, I felt like I was wearing guilt like a stone gargoyle on my back. It pulled me down and made everything feel like it took too much energy. Nora was never a silver lining, plucky, glass-half-full type of person. She'd always gone through these dark moods; they were like sucking black holes. If you got too close, tried to cheer her up, she'd pull you in until you felt as miserable as she did. There was no jollying her out of one of her funks. It was one of the reasons that we'd drifted apart. I got sick of it, and now she was dead.

Last year in health class we had a unit on the warning signs of suicide. Even as I wrote them down in my notebook so I could memorize them for the test, I shifted uncomfortably in my seat, thinking how many of them sounded like Nora. I never said anything. Not to her, not to our lame school counselor, her parents, or mine. I just filed away the fact that it sounded like her and moved on. Then the night of the party I knew something was wrong. The whole story about someone conning her, her giving away her notebook, the way she hugged me when we said good-bye. Something was off. I ignored it because I wanted to go back to my house and talk to my friends about Colton.

My last conversation with Nora outside the party only three days ago kept playing in my head, making me feel like throwing up. I would close my eyes at night and see her standing there, thanking me, and then me walking away. I kept waiting for someone to stick a finger in my face and scream that I was the one who let her die, demanding I take responsibility for failing her. I could picture people recoiling from me in disgust when they heard. I could imagine my parents' faces if they knew, how disappointed they would be in me. Part of me was dreading others finding out, and the other part wanted someone to do it, so it could all be out in the open. Instead my parents were tiptoeing around me, making a point to tell me how much they loved me. Even my friends who had never liked Nora had gone out of their way to be extra nice to me. Calling to say how bad they felt.

I hadn't gone to school for the past two days and instead hid in my bedroom. The shocking thing was that my parents let me get away with it. Normally our family rules required a fever, a notarized note from a doctor, and a possible case of Ebola before I could stay home from school. Anything short of bleeding or active death was dealt with by giving out some Tylenol and one of those mini packs of tissues. The problem was I couldn't hide anymore. Today was Nora's funeral, and there was no escaping the fact I was expected to show up.

"Are you ready?" Mom asked. She stood in the doorway to my room, but she seemed almost afraid to enter. She was wearing one of her black suits from work. I wondered if every time I saw her wearing it after this I would think, *That's the suit she wore to Nora's funeral.*

"I guess."

"Ms. Heady called this morning."

I went completely still. I wondered if Nora's mom had called to say I wasn't welcome at the funeral. That if I couldn't be there for Nora when it mattered, I had no business showing up at her memorial service.

"She's going to have a part in the service where they will invite people from the congregation to share a memory of Nora."

"Do I have to say anything?" My skin turned clammy. What if I started blabbing about all kinds of random stuff? I could talk about the time when we read her mom's Harlequin romance novels out loud and made a list of the terms used to describe a penis. Her favorite was "he unleashed his pink steel." Sure, that would be a great story I could tell everyone in their moment of grief. Or I could tell them about the time that I had called her in a panic because I was pretty sure I had lost a tampon somewhere inside me, and she had to talk me down so we could figure out what to do. Or the time we snuck into her parents' liquor cabinet and drank a bottle of crème de menthe we found way in the back and ended up throwing up, and how I still couldn't eat a Peppermint Pattie without feeling vaguely nauseated. I could picture myself standing there completely unable to think of a single appropriate memory to tell the crowd.

Or maybe I could talk about how I blew her off when she needed me most.

"No, of course you don't have to speak at the service if you don't want to," Mom said. "Ms. Heady knows this is a hard time for you. She just wanted to let you know in case you needed a bit of time to think of something. She didn't want you to feel put on the spot."

"I should say something, though, shouldn't I? Everyone will expect me to." I tried to swallow, but all the saliva in my mouth seemed to have dried up. I felt a bit light-headed.

Mom rested a hand on my shoulder. "You don't have to do anything that doesn't feel comfortable." She squeezed my arm.

"Your dad and I are downstairs when you're ready."

After she left, I glanced down at my desk. I'd buried the notebook Nora had given me in my bottom desk drawer. I'd piled heavy binders and books on top of it as if I thought it was going to crawl on its own, zombie style, out of the drawer. I hadn't looked at it. I was afraid of what she might have written in there. Over the past three days I'd been sure someone would ask me about what she'd given me. Maybe even the police would show up and want it as some kind of evidence, but no one brought it up. I stood and looked myself over in the mirror. I picked a piece of lint off the sleeve of the dress my mom had lent me. I thought I looked older. Like a thousand years older.

I didn't have a vast amount of funeral experience. Understatement. The only other funeral I'd ever been to was my grandfather's when I was twelve. I'm not sure it even counts as a funeral, since my grandma kept calling it a "celebration of life" instead. Everyone at the event, other than me and my parents, was old. Really old, not just parent old.

The first thing I noticed when we walked into Nora's family church was how young everyone was. It could have been a school assembly, except for the organ music and how everyone was dressed up. The lack of cheerleaders and hand-painted signs was also a clue. I might have imagined it, but it seemed like the quiet church grew even more silent as my parents and I walked up the aisle. Her parents asked us to sit near the front since I had been Nora's closest friend. I'd flinched when my parents told me that. Nora and I hadn't really hung out as friends since high school started. I didn't blow her off in the hallway, and we'd gotten together a few times, but I wouldn't have listed her as one my close friends. Now I felt even guiltier that she hadn't replaced me along the way. I was glad when we finally got to our seats, so I could stop feeling like a huge spotlight was following me down the aisle.

Nora's dad led his new wife to a pew at the front. His face was locked down, reminding me more of a mannequin than a real person. Nora's stepmom had dark circles under her eyes and bright, almost fluorescent, red lipstick. She was clearly in the camp that felt changes in a woman's body should be celebrated and wore a tight, body-hugging black dress that did everything to accentuate her pregnancy short of one of those arrows pointing to her belly with the words "bun in the oven" printed across the top.

I felt a snicker bubble up inside me. I could imagine Nora's voice in my head.

She's wearing that to my funeral? Christ on a pogo stick, did she think the service was being held at her gynecologist's office? If that dress was any shorter, I could do a pelvic exam from here. I swear to God, if she drops that baby during my funeral, I will haunt her for eternity.

I turned around to see Nora's mom coming up the aisle.

Nora's two aunts flanked her, holding on to her elbows. She looked shell-shocked. Her eyes kept darting around, glancing at everyone. I sensed she half expected Nora to pop up and yell out, "Surprise!"

Over the church loudspeakers a popular ballad that was always on the radio started to play. Nora would have hated it. She preferred the really alternative stuff, lots of bass. *If you've heard it, I've already moved on to something else,* she used to say. A few girls from school started to cry. Nora would have *really* hated that. They weren't even people she hung out with. I realized my hands were shaking and sat on them to keep them still.

Pallbearers guided the highly polished casket down the aisle to the front of the church. It gave me a jolt of panic. For some reason I hadn't expected Nora to be here. Course, technically this was her party; she was the guest of honor, so to speak. The urge to laugh started to bubble up again, and I bit the inside of my cheek to make it stop.

There was a spray of white roses on top of the casket. Someone had arranged for a framed copy of her senior picture to be propped up alongside. It was a good picture, but it didn't look like her. Too polished. She had what she called her beauty pageant smile on. I suspected she'd lost a fight with her mom about what to wear for the photo.

I had the sudden urge to run for it. I spun around to see how far I was from the door. That's when I saw Brody. He was sitting near the back by himself. He was still and stoic. Like a statue you'd see in Washington, DC. There were dark circles under his eyes, and it looked like he'd lost weight. He met my eyes through the crowd and nodded. His nod was more than recognition that he saw me. It was like he reached through the air and whispered in my ear that it was okay and that I could do this. I nodded back at him and took a deep breath before turning around. I'd run out on Nora once. This time I owed it to her to stay.

chapter seven

I didn't understand why there had to be a social event after a funeral. I'd never felt less like having a party. Nora's parents had arranged to have food brought into the church social hall. It looked like a cheap wedding reception. There were flowers that were already starting to go limp on the tables and a buffet table at the front with those silver warming dishes. People were dressed up, but a few had slipped off their uncomfortable shoes, and several of the guys had hung their suit jackets on the backs of their folding chairs and loosened their ties. Nora's mom sat on one side of the room and her dad and his wife on the other. They shared a daughter, but they weren't going to share this experience. People milled in between the two or hung out in groups, chatting. There were even people laughing here and there.

I'd mumbled how sorry I was to Nora's mom, but I couldn't say that she heard me. She stared through me. She had a grip on my hand. Her skin was ice cold. It was like she was the dead one. I had to tug my hand free when I walked away.

I glanced around, but Brody must have left after the service. I wasn't sure why I wanted to see him. It wasn't as if he and I were friends, but I wanted to talk to someone else who had known her. I wanted to ask him if he'd noticed that she was acting unusual that night. Maybe if he had, we could split the guilt; I wasn't sure I could carry it all on my own.

The idea of eating something made me nauseated, but I was thirsty. I went to the front of the hall and took a cup of punch. It was super sweet. I could feel the sugar molecules knitting furry little sweaters for each of my teeth.

Shannon and Lydia made a beeline for me through the crowd.

"How are you?" Lydia asked, with her eyes scrunched up in concern.

"Did your mom tell you I stopped by?" Shannon reached out and touched my arm.

"The whole thing is horrible. I can't even believe it." Lydia had pulled her hair back into a tight bun with not a single hair out of place. She looked like her mother.

"Hey, listen, I talked to the yearbook staff." Shannon was one of the editors in addition to her other extracurricular activities. "We're going to do a two-page spread on Nora in the senior section."

Our conversation didn't seem to require my input at all. I sipped the sticky, sweet punch and faked an interest I didn't feel in layout ideas.

A group of sophomore girls approached slowly. "We came to say we're sorry about what happened," the tallest one said to me.

"Thanks," Shannon replied.

"We're still in shock," Lydia added. Her eyes welled up with tears.

I stared at Lydia. I couldn't remember her and Nora ever having more than a two-minute conversation with each other. The way Lydia was acting, they had been besties for years. I wanted to point this out, but it didn't really matter. I wasn't in any position to slam anyone else for not being a good friend to Nora.

"She had so much ahead of her, so many opportunities." Shannon sighed. "I've been reading up on teen suicide. Did you know it's the third leading cause of death in people in our age group? That's just wrong."

When had Shannon become a public service announcement?

"I e-mailed Mr. Bradshaw. I think the school should look at setting up some kind of peer counseling options."

"You talked to the guidance counselor about this?" I asked. The idea of Shannon and Mr. Bradshaw cooking up some teen crisis hotline annoyed me for some reason. Part of it was I hated Bradshaw. He was always trying to act hip and cool, as if he was one of our peers who just happened to work for the school administration. He used way too much hair product and cologne. Being near him gave me a headache. You could also tell he'd been a hugger, but someone had complained. In today's day and age, being a creepy older guy who liked to hug teens was frowned upon. He'd stopped touching students, but you could tell he still wanted to. Instead what he did now was whenever he got close he would clap you firmly on the back. It was like a halfhearted Heimlich maneuver. He also had this nervous tic where he would pinch his lips together, like he was about to kiss you. It made him look a bit like a guppy. His nickname in the halls was Fishman.

"A lot of teens don't feel they can talk to an adult. They want someone who can relate, another student who gets what they're going through," Shannon said.

I raised an eyebrow. Why anyone would feel more comfortable talking to another student was a mystery to me. Not to mention, I was quite sure that Nora wouldn't have thought anyone in our class could relate to her. "Were you going to ask me about it?" There was an edge in my voice. Lydia and Shannon exchanged a glance. The sophomore girls were staring at me with wide eyes, like they expected me to flip the buffet table over and throw a fit.

"I didn't think it would upset you." Shannon's voice was flat and calm. How someone might respond to a crazy person who was yelling things at them on the street. "I wanted to do something that would help. You know, to keep this from happening to anyone else."

I clenched my teeth to avoid saying anything I couldn't take back. I didn't need any more regrets. I looked across the room and saw Colton standing with a bunch of the guys from the football team.

"Excuse me," I mumbled. I pushed through the crowd until I was at his side.

"Hey." Colton shoved his hands in his pockets. I'd hoped he would toss his arm around my shoulder and anchor me, but he didn't touch me. Maybe part of the "taking a break" rules included a no-contact clause. His friends started to move off.

"See you at Pete's," one of them said as he turned away.

My face tensed. "You guys are going to Pinball Pete's? Now?" Pete's was an arcade full of old video games, cheap pool tables, and foosball in a basement store near the Michigan State campus. Their pink-elephant sign was the only way you'd spot it. The poor lighting was probably to keep you from noticing how grungy the place was. The bathroom looked like you could catch hepatitis if you were in there for too long.

He shrugged. "The teachers told us to take the rest of the day off."

I stared at him. "So you're going to play games." He just stared at me. "You don't think that's . . ." I searched for the right word. Disrespectful, rude, disgusting. "Wrong?"

"We're here now." Colton looked around the room. "How long are we supposed to stay at this thing?"

"It's not about putting in your time, it's about the fact that it's the day of Nora's funeral. Funerals and foosball don't go together." I was trying to whisper, but my voice must have been louder than I imagined, because a few people at the tables near us were turning around.

"What am I supposed to do, just hang out all day being sad?"

"She's dead. Is it really asking too much that you take a single day to, I don't know, acknowledge that she lived?" I wanted to throw my glass of punch in his face.

"Why are you on my case? I didn't even know her that well. I came here because I thought you would want me to be here and now you jump all over me."

"Am I supposed to thank you for your great sacrifice? You really put yourself out." My chest was turning a mottled red, and my skin felt hot and itchy. Suddenly it hit me: He and his friends had only come because it gave them an excuse to skip class. Heck, that's probably why most people were here.

"What do you want from me?" Colton and I were nearly nose-to-nose.

I opened my mouth to yell something back, but nothing came out. I was mad at Shannon and Lydia for acting like they cared, and mad at Colton for not acting like he cared enough. My breath started to come faster. My mouth kept opening and closing. Suddenly my throat seized, and I started crying for the first time since I'd heard the news.

Colton's eyes went wide. "Hey, it's okay." He looked around nervously. He reached over to pat my back, but his hand just hovered a few inches away from me as if he was afraid to touch me.

I started crying harder. It wasn't okay. It wasn't remotely okay at all. Colton took a step back, and I reached for him to grab hold of his shirt. I wanted to explain how everything was wrong. This couldn't be happening. It wasn't possible that Nora was dead.

Lydia and Shannon came running over and surrounded me. They made soft murmuring comments and rubbed my shoulders. I tried to pull myself together, but I couldn't stop crying. More and more people were turning around to see what was happening. I could feel them staring at me. I wanted to explain that what I felt was real; it wasn't a show. I wanted to explain that I'd never been so sorry about anything in my entire life as I was about this.

My mom appeared at my side and took my arm. "Okay, honey, come on."

"She just started crying," Colton said as he backed farther away from me. He seemed grateful to pass me over to my mom. "I didn't say anything."

"It's time for us to head home," Mom said. I went limp, the tears cutting off. If it had been possible, I would have crawled into her arms and let her carry me out of there.

"We're all so upset about what happened to Nora," Lydia said to my mom. "If there's anything we can do to help . . ." Everyone grew silent. It seemed clear even to me that I needed far more help than they could give me.

My dad brought over my mom's purse. "I'll go get the car and pull it around," he said to my mom. He squeezed my elbow before leaving.

Mom pulled a crumpled Kleenex out of her bag and blotted my face.

"I'm so tired," I said softly.

"We're going to take you home."

I let her lead me to the door. People around us were quiet as we left. I guess my little breakdown was the entertainment for the funeral. Not as much fun as a band, but certainly more memorable.

We walked outside and I stopped short. The sun had come out while we had been inside. The light bounced off the wet leaves lying in the street, and the puddles in the parking lot gave off a glare. Despite the sunshine it was cold. The sky was a brilliant blue, and the air felt razor sharp when I breathed in. It was painfully beautiful.

chapter eight

The next morning was a real eye-opener. Teen magazines are always offering advice on how to be popular. They suggest getting involved in sports, or spending extra time on your hair or makeup. There was always the advice that the most important thing was to be confident and friendly. Smile. Express interest in others.

Bullshit.

Apparently the secret to popularity here at Northside High is to kill yourself. Nora had always been on the fringes. She wasn't unpopular. Her status was hard to explain. No one shoved her into her locker or pushed her down in gym. If anything, other people were a little bit scared of her. They tended to give her a wide berth when she'd been around. However, now that she was dead, she'd reached near demigod status. Her locker had become a shrine, with people leaving fake flowers stuck into the vent. Someone had scrawled a quote about memories living forever in Sharpie marker on the door. There was even a tacky baby-blue stuffed bear left leaning against the locker. Her Facebook page, which she almost never bothered to update, was now full of comments about how she'd be missed and cheesy quotes from various songs that she'd never liked. Nora's name seemed to be on everyone's lips.

People were still buzzing about what had happened. They were like emotional vampires, sucking up the drama. Who hasn't stood on a balcony and realized that there was nothing to stop them from jumping over? Or been driving and suddenly realized that they could slam on the gas and head straight into traffic? Not that you wanted to die, but the realization that you could was somehow intoxicating. Dangerous. Nora had taken the plunge, and everyone was fascinated. Nora had been telling elaborate stories for years. If she'd been doing it for attention, she sure had it now. Too bad she wasn't around to see it.

Shannon and Lydia had stayed glued to my side my first day back as if I required security to keep away hordes of paparazzi. I wanted to believe that they were doing this because they were my friends, but I couldn't escape the feeling that they liked being close to the center of the action.

Colton had made it a point to stop by my locker first thing in the morning and bring me a coffee from Starbucks. I could hear girls in the hallway sigh and buzz over the fact that we might be getting back together.

"Thanks." I took a sip of the latte. He'd forgotten to add sugar.

"Things with you okay?" Colton asked.

"I'm doing better." I smiled so he would relax and realize I wasn't about to fly apart like I had at the funeral. "You want to get out of here for lunch? We could do Maloney's, my treat." I figured I owed him one.

Colton shifted, staring down at his feet. "I don't think that would be a good idea. You know, since we're on a break."

Lydia was looking at me from across the hall with pain in her eyes. She felt sorry for me. It was as obvious as if she'd taken out a full-page ad in the school paper. I flushed.

"Fine. No big deal." Now even Colton was looking at me with sympathy, which annoyed me. I wouldn't have said anything to him if he hadn't approached me first. It wasn't like there were guidelines about how we were supposed to act around each other. "I just thought I'd pay you back for the coffee," I explained.

"I really care about you, but I still think we need some space," Colton said. "I brought you the coffee because I knew today would be hard."

I wanted to tell him not to do me any favors, but I wasn't interested in having a fight in the middle of the hallway. "Well, thanks again." What did he want me to say? It was coffee. It wasn't like he gave me his liver or something. He shuffled off down the hall with his friends.

"He'll come around," Lydia said, rushing to my side. "I talked to Karl and he said Colton still talks about you all the time. He's just being a guy." She shook her head as if the mysteries of the male creature were too much to fathom.

"It's fine. We both thought it was a good idea to take a break."

"Sure, of course," Shannon said, sounding like she didn't believe me at all.

"I really like Colton, but he's never been the love of my life." I didn't care that we were on a break. What bothered me was trying to figure out how we were supposed to act with each other now. We were still part of the same crowd, and neither of us was likely to leave. Even though it had been mutual, for some reason he seemed to be getting the role of the breaker-upper, leaving me to the sad, tragic dumpee. I stared back at both of them. "You guys, I'm fine."

Lydia patted my back softly. "Of course you are. You're more than fine."

"I have to go," I said. I had to see our cheer coach. I hadn't been looking forward to talking to her, but now I was glad to have an excuse to leave.

It's a little-known fact that the correct term is "pom*pon*," not "pom-pom." I know these details because Coach Kerr takes running our cheer squad as seriously as operating a nuclear power plant. If she catches you calling it a pom-pom, or in some way not taking our glorious sport with the level of gravity it deserves, she makes the entire squad run extra laps. This doesn't exactly make you popular with everyone.

I'd gotten the message from Coach Kerr, asking me to see her, in homeroom. She didn't need to sign it; there was no mistaking the note was from her. She still dotted her *i*'s with small bubbles. It seemed once you were over thirty, there should be a rule about not doing that anymore. No wonder she made Liz our alternate on the squad—they had handwriting in common. Calling her space an office was a bit of a stretch. I'm pretty sure it used to be a janitor's closet until she demanded that the administration give her a room of her own. She'd covered the walls with those annoying motivational posters. I wondered if she ever got tired of being so perky all the time. Coach Kerr was originally from Texas, where cheerleading was practically a religion. I think she found Michigan disappointing on many levels: our weather, the fact we didn't wear our hair as large as she did, the quality of our barbecue, and that people didn't see cheering as a divine calling.

"Ah, Miss Scott, how are you?" She arranged her face into what passed as a frowny face for her. She'd had a lot of work done, and expressions weren't exactly her strength. Her face tended to look stiff, like a Disney princess Halloween mask. "I hope you know the entire squad has been pulling for you. I know losing someone you know, especially at this age, can be hard." She pressed her lips together and shook her head sadly.

I thought of pointing out that I hadn't lost Nora; it wasn't a case where she'd wandered off at the zoo—she was dead—but I knew that wasn't a discussion Coach Kerr was interested in having. Dead wasn't perky. "Thanks. Everyone's been great."

"Do you feel like getting back to it?"

My nose twitched from the smell of her perfume. The day after Nora's funeral there had been a playoff football game. I hadn't been in any shape to show up, yelling on the sidelines for people to get fired up. The idea of standing there while we had some meaningless moment of silence for Nora had made me sick. My mom had called and made an excuse for me.

"I'm not sure I'm ready," I said.

Her lips pursed. It wasn't the answer she wanted, but it's tacky to give someone a hassle right after you told her you understood how she was going through a difficult time.

"Since we lost the game, there's a break before basketball starts," I said. She frowned. I sounded entirely too happy that the football season had ended in glorious defeat. "If I could have just a bit more time, it would help."

Coach Kerr opened her mouth, but I cut her off. "I always knew I could count on you to understand."

A satisfied smile spread across her face. Coach Kerr was obsessed with being a part of our squad. She was always talking about how some actor our age was really hot, or how much she liked some new band, in an effort to be one of us. Coach talked about how we should think of her like an older sister. No one mentioned that she was the same age as our moms, and she was entirely too boot-camp sergeant for us to consider her a friend.

"Of course I understand," she said. She shuffled the papers on her desk, tapping them into a tidy pile. "You're right. There's a natural break here. Take a week or two for yourself." Coach wagged a finger at me. "If we don't take care of ourselves, no one else will."

I nodded. I didn't bother telling her that worrying only about myself is exactly how I'd gotten into this situation.

chapter nine

My parents forced me to make an appointment to see Bradshaw. They thought it was important I had someone I could talk to, despite the fact I tried telling them he was the last person I would want to share my feelings with. I sat in his office, rolling the hem of my sweater between my fingers.

"It's normal to feel upset," he said. His lips went in and out, in full-on guppy-face mode. Fishman on speed.

I tried not to roll my eyes. This was the best our school could do? It seemed to me if someone went to grad school and got to have a fancy nameplate on their door, they should be able to offer better advice than "it's normal to feel upset." Thanks, Captain Obvious.

He sighed. "Your folks told me about how your early application to Duke wasn't accepted. I also heard about you and

Colton." He made an exaggerated sad face like some kind of annoying circus clown.

I sat up straighter. What had he heard?

"Colton came in to talk to me. He felt bad about what happened between the two of you, especially with you losing Nora the very next day. He knows how important Duke is to you." Bradshaw tapped his pen on the desk. If he expected me to say something, he was going to wait a long time. I could kill Colton for talking to Bradshaw. If he felt bad, he could have told me instead, or spilled his guts to Karl, or one of his other friends. Did he really have to take it to Northside's version of Dr. Phil? "I think Colton's worried that between losing Nora, the news about Duke, and then the break with him, it could leave you feeling . . . upset. Now, I get how it might seem like everything is crashing in on you. No one would want you to do anything to yourself."

My mouth fell open. "You think I'd kill myself over Colton?" Did people really think he was so great that without him I'd fall apart? We weren't even officially broken up, unless Colton had forgotten to mention that part to me.

"No, I'm not saying that. I meant more because of everything happening at once, you might be overwhelmed. Sometimes when things are going bad, people make bad decisions." He shook his head sadly. He was still waiting for me to deny it.

"I'm not thinking about killing myself." I tried to ignore the fact that he was implying that my life was so pathetic that it might seem reasonable to me to end it. "I'm fine. I told my parents I was going to be okay. I got upset at the funeral, but I'm doing better now."

"Your parents are worried about you, huh?" He gave a chuffing sound. "Parents can drive you nuts sometimes."

Great. Now we were buddies in this together. Then I saw Brody. He was standing by the closed door to the office. There was a pane of glass, about a foot wide, that ran alongside the door. Brody pressed his face to the glass when he recognized me.

"My parents have been great," I said, trying to ignore Brody. I could imagine what Nora would do if she was here. She'd start telling Bradshaw stories, things about how she was a cutter or was being bullied for being gay. Anything to get him all riled up and excited. She'd string him along just for her own amusement.

"Well, that's good. You need to know that you're going to feel many things over the next bit. Lots of ups and downs." He waved his hand like it was a roller coaster.

I glanced over. Brody puckered up his mouth, doing a perfect Fishman impression. I pressed my mouth together to keep from laughing.

"Avery?"

My head spun around. Bradshaw was looking at me, his guppy lips pooching in and out. Uh-oh. He must have said something that required an answer. "Sorry," I mumbled. "I was just thinking about how lucky I am that you're so willing to listen. It's hard to find an adult who isn't judgmental."

A person with an ounce of insight would have realized that I was laying it on thick, but Bradshaw wasn't known for his keen ability to smell sarcasm. He actually believed that the students all loved him. He and Coach Kerr should date. I stood up to leave and he came around his desk. There was a moment when I thought he was going to break the strict no-hugging rule, but then he settled for one of his bracing slaps on the back. He slapped my back so hard I thought my spine was going to fly out of my mouth.

"Now, my door is always open. Remember what I said."

"It's okay to be upset," I said as I opened his door.

"And to expect the ups and downs." He gave my back another whack. I was going to need a chiropractor to realign my spine when this meeting was over.

"I sure will."

Brody leaned against the wall in the hallway outside the office. I could feel the hum of excitement in Bradshaw's voice when he spotted him. He likely dreamed of students seeking him out versus being forced to make an appointment.

"Brody! Good to see you." He held out a closed hand so they could fist-bump. This was Bradshaw's way of keeping it real. Brody paused for a moment and I thought he might leave him hanging there, but in the end he halfheartedly met Bradshaw's fist with his own.

"You sent me a note saying I was supposed to see you," Brody said.

Bradshaw suddenly clapped his hands together, making the both of us jump. "I just had a brilliant idea!"

Neither Brody nor I said anything, but I had the feeling he was as skeptical about this brilliant idea as I was.

"Brody, I brought you down so we could talk about your senior project, and now that I see the two of you together, it clicked." He slapped both of us on the back. Brody and I looked at each other warily. Bradshaw looked entirely too excited, like someone selling religion. "Avery is looking for a new partner for her project too."

I opened my mouth to protest, and then closed it with a click. If Colton felt the need to tell Bradshaw that he was worried I was going to hurl myself into traffic or start drinking Drano cocktails, then odds were our break was a lot more like a breakup. Brody's need for a new partner for his project was a bit more obvious. When I looked over at Brody, he shrugged slightly, which I decided to take that he wasn't repulsed by the idea.

"Yeah. I guess," I said.

"Okay! Everybody high-five." He pumped his hand in the air. Brody and I both limply slapped his hand so that the horror could end. "Now you two hunker in and figure out what you want to do and let me know. I'm rooting for you guys."

He bustled back into his office, leaving us standing there looking at each other.

chapter ten

I waited until Bradshaw closed the door to his office and then punched Brody in the arm.

"What's that for?" Brody rubbed his bicep.

"For almost making me laugh in there. The guy already thinks I'm on the edge. If I'd started laughing in the middle of his 'we're all in this together, isn't the world a great place' speech, he was going to have me locked up. I was trying to at least look like I was listening to him, and you're out here making fish faces."

"I couldn't resist. He had me in for a heart-to-heart on Monday, just so he could tell me that real men aren't afraid to cry."

"He didn't," I said.

"Oh yes he did. He said, and I'm quoting here, 'Batman

wouldn't have existed without pain and emotion.'" Brody's lip curled up in a half smile. "I think he was actively disappointed that I didn't break down right then and there, vowing to take up a life as a secret hero vigilante to avenge Nora."

"Wow."

"Can you imagine what Nora would have said?" Brody asked.

I burst out laughing and Brody joined me. I hadn't laughed in days and it felt unnatural, the sound almost fake as it came out of my mouth. Brody did his lip impression of Bradshaw again and I laughed harder, it coming easier the second time.

"You're a fish-faced Batman," I said.

Brody placed his hand on his hips, giving himself a hero stance. "Enemy of evil, protector of truth, justice, the American way, and the right to shed a few manly tears now and then." He looked around. "You want to get something to eat?"

I glanced at the clock. "I've got calculus next period. I can't miss it."

Brody smiled. "No problem." He started down the hall and after a few steps paused, looking back at me. "You coming?"

I followed him down to the empty cafeteria. "They're not open," I pointed out.

He held up a finger. "Not for the average person, but I think we've established that I'm a vigilante and outside the law." He motioned to the open kitchen. "Go up and ask them something."

"What am I supposed to say?"

Brody sighed. "I don't know. I need a distraction. Ask them

about getting a recipe or something." He pushed me toward the kitchen window before I could figure out why he needed the distraction.

"Excuse me!" The three cooks looked up from what they were doing. "Can I ask you ladies something?" They wiped their hands on towels and came closer to the window. Behind them I saw the side door open and Brody slip into the kitchen.

"We're not open until the first lunch break," one said.

"I know. I wondered if you could answer some questions about your recipes? I have a friend who's allergic to gluten," I babbled. I tried to look at the cooks, but I could see Brody behind them, grabbing a couple of cookies off a cooling rack and two cartons of milk. "Gluten's in everything, so I want to make sure she doesn't get sick."

"There's a printout on food allergies in the office." The cook started to turn back. I lunged forward and grabbed her arm. All three of them looked at me.

"I, uh, just wanted to thank you. For caring . . . about food allergies. It means everything."

"Sure." The cook tried to pull out of my grasp.

"Food feeds the body, but the love you put in the food feeds the soul."

I saw the cooks exchange a glance. They thought I might be on something. "Well, that's great." The cook took a step back so I couldn't reach her. I saw the side door swing shut.

"Okay, thanks!" I hustled out.

Brody was just outside the cafeteria, laughing. "Feed the soul?"

I grabbed the cookie out of his hand. "I had to improvise. I can't believe you stole from the cafeteria."

"Lighten up. It's a cookie; I didn't raid the cash box." He tossed me a milk carton and slid down the closest locker so he was sitting. "Cookies are warm," he said, taking a bite.

The smell of warm chocolate and sugar was irresistible. I sat down on the floor next to him. "I didn't know you and Nora were friends until the party," I said.

"I used to go to the camera store where she worked. We started talking, and then after that we started hanging out sometimes."

I was trying to figure out how to ask if they'd dated. Brody glanced at me and must have been able to read my mind.

"We were just friends. We both liked taking pictures. Nora was clear she wasn't looking to date. She was pretty antirelationship since her folks busted up."

"You're a photographer?"

Brody shrugged. "I try."

"What kind of pictures?"

"A bit of everything." He licked a smear of chocolate off the side of his finger. "Sounds vague, doesn't it? I'm not trying to be secretive; I just don't know how to explain it. The camera lets me see things in a different way. It's like I finally have perspective. I can't always say stuff right in words. Pictures are easier."

"I like writing," I said. My mouth clicked shut. I wasn't sure where that had come from.

"I know." He must have seen the surprise in my eyes. "Nora told me. She said you guys used to write stuff together, but you were the good one."

I waved away his compliment. "We wrote stupid stuff, for laughs."

"I don't know. Being able to make people laugh doesn't seem stupid to me."

I looked away. I was embarrassed that he knew I wrote. It felt like I had accidentally shown him naked pictures of myself. "It's just a hobby. It's not like it's something I could do as a job."

"People do. I mean, it's not easy, but if it's what you really wanted to do, you could find a way."

"It's not what I want to do." My voice came out harsher than I intended.

Brody's eyebrows went up. "Okay. I wasn't planning to force you into the life of a starving author or anything."

There was nothing I couldn't screw up lately. I couldn't even let people be nice to me. "Sorry."

"It's okay. You're most likely a bit unstable these days. You should expect to have your feelings go up and down a lot over the next few weeks."

I looked up at Brody, and he was doing the Bradshaw guppy face again.

"He gave you the same talk, huh?" I guessed.

"He's probably got a manual that contains heart-to-heart talks for all these types of situations. I think you should be disappointed he didn't tell you how you could be Batman. Sort of sexist, really." Brody shook his head sadly.

"He might have been telling me that I could be Wonder Woman, but I was distracted by the faces you were making."

"My turn to be sorry." He tipped back the milk and finished it off in one go. "You okay with the idea of being partners for the project?"

Did he want to get out of it? "I guess. You?"

"Sure. I mean, if you do. What were you and Colton doing?"

I thought about asking what he'd heard about Colton and me, but maybe not knowing how the rest of Northside's student body was dissecting my social life was a good thing. "We were planning to do an analysis on school reform." Brody raised a single eyebrow, and I felt a flush of irritation. "It's very topical. There's all sorts of stuff in the news about it."

"Yeah, sure."

"I'm applying to Duke. I need to have an impressive project." Northside required everyone to do a senior project, from those who were college bound, to seniors who were already majoring in smoking weed and underperforming. Because everyone had to do them, some of the projects were fairly lame. As long as you picked a topic, did at least some research, and stood up and talked about what you learned for the required ten minutes, you passed. "Nora told me you guys were looking for her mom for your project."

"Her idea."

"That doesn't surprise me. Looking for her mom has been a project of Nora's for a long time." I realized what I'd said. "Had been a project."

"She's a hard person to think about in the past tense."

Both of us were quiet for a moment. I finished my cookie. "How were you helping her? In addition to your Batman crime-solving skills, do you also hunt down missing persons?"

"Batman was always more than mere brawn," Brody pointed out. "Nora did most of the investigating. She wrote everything down in this notebook. It was like she was preparing for battle. I was more of a sounding board. I was taking pictures as we went. Sort of documentary style. Stuff that would hopefully show different kinds of families. Something we could show for the talk in case we didn't find her mom."

"She must have been over the moon when she thought she had." I tried to imagine how happy she must have been before it all went downhill.

"I knew something about the whole thing was off. I'm the one who convinced her it could be a con and to check it out before things went any further. I knew it would upset her, but I didn't think—" He didn't finish his sentence.

"How did you figure it out? That Carla was a con, I mean."

He tossed his milk carton into the trash can across the hall.

It went in with a swoosh. "I never thought we'd find her mom. There wasn't enough to go on. She didn't have a name or anything. There wasn't any formal paperwork that had any clues. She didn't even know her exact birthday. The convent that took her in as a baby guessed she was a couple of weeks old and just picked a date. They picked May thirtieth because it was Joan of Arc's feast day." He shook his head. "Then when this woman showed up, Carla, it all fit together too neat. I didn't buy it."

"If you knew you wouldn't find her mom, why did you agree to do the project?"

"Nora wanted to," Brody said simply.

I took a deep breath. "So, looking for her mom is out, and I'm guessing Colton's going to want to keep the education topic to himself, so that's a non-option. What do you think we should do?"

"Screw Colton. He doesn't get to choose. Do you want to do education as our project?"

I flushed. I liked the way he pushed Colton's wants out of the picture without even worrying about it. "Do *you*?"

He looked appalled. "God, no. Nothing personal, but it sounds boring as shit."

I laughed. "It was kind of boring."

Brody broke into a smile. "Perfect. Education reform is out. Opens up all sorts of ideas."

"Like?"

"Zombies. History of Batman." His eyes sparkled. "We

could toss in Wonder Woman too, but if you want my opinion, there are more interesting superheroes to choose from. Iron Man is very trendy at the moment. Aquaman is vastly overlooked—one of the founders of the Justice League, you know."

"Can't say I did. Nothing against Aquaman, but I'm not sure Duke would be impressed. They already turned me down once, so I need to make this project good." My stomach tightened just thinking about it. Somewhere in North Carolina there was an admissions counselor with the ability to give me my life back or hurl me under a bus.

"Why do you want them if they don't want you? If you ask me, they're a waste of your energy."

His comment threw me and for a beat I didn't answer. "They're the best. I need to go there. It's not an option."

Brody didn't look convinced. "Whatever."

The bell rang, and classroom doors flew open and people thundered out. Brody stood and pulled me up onto my feet. He took my empty milk carton from me and dumped it in the trash.

I saw Lydia and Shannon making a beeline for me so they could resume their security patrol. "We don't need to pick a topic now," I said. "I'll call you."

Brody listed off his number while I put it in my cell. "I'll wait to hear from you." He held out his fist and gave me an ironic smile. "Until then: Strength, Power, Courage." He must have seen my confusion. "Justice League motto, also not bad for surviving high school."

I fist-bumped him back. "Strength, Power, Courage."

I watched him disappear into the crowd of people.

"What did *he* want?" Shannon asked when she reached my side.

"Bradshaw partnered us up for the senior project."

Shannon and Lydia exchanged a look. "Maybe we can see if you can join us. There are a few other groups of three."

As much as I like my two best friends, the idea of working on their project gave me hives. Part of it was their topic— Fat: Friend or Foe—on the difference between healthy and unhealthy fats. Spending months making a presentation that showed smiling avocados and salmon and evil greasy-looking bags of chips seemed like a punishment. Not to mention I didn't think knowing the exact fat count of a single Wheat Thin was going to convince Duke they needed to sign me up. Then there was the fact that there was something about Brody that made me feel relaxed. I wanted to do the project with him.

"You know how Bradshaw is." I shook my head like I couldn't get over how annoying he could be. "I'm pretty much stuck with Brody."

"What are you guys going to do for a project?"

"I don't know." As soon as the words were out of my mouth, the idea came to me, and I jolted like I'd been poked with a live wire. It was perfect.

chapter eleven

I didn't tell Brody my idea right away, although I wanted to. The idea was like this expanding balloon inside of me that was swelling every second, and soon I wouldn't be able to contain it. I practically was bouncing off the walls by the time school was over and I could get home. Lydia and Shannon wanted me to go out with them, but I begged off, telling them I was still pretty wiped from everything. As soon as I got home, I pounded up the stairs and shut my bedroom door behind me, even though I was home alone and the chance of anyone busting in on me was pretty much impossible.

I pulled open the desk drawer and carefully slid out Nora's notebook as if it might bite. The paper cover was so worn that it felt soft, almost like fabric. My fingers traced the words on the front: *Field Guide to Finding Your Family*. I suddenly had an image that the inside of the notebook would be blank, the words I'd seen earlier at the party gone, like she'd written the entire thing in disappearing ink. I opened the cover and almost dropped it when I saw my name. I had a hard time focusing at first, but then I realized it was because my hands were shaking, making it hard to read.

Hi Avery,

Remember in sixth grade when we had to read "The Diary of Anne Frank" in English class and we decided we wanted to have our own diaries? Both of us quit after a few weeks because it turned out we really didn't have much happening in our lives worth writing down. I couldn't imagine that generations of readers would be riveted to know what we had for dinner, or that I was pretty sure that Ryan in my science class had looked at my butt. This was the downside to not living through a war as a refugee hiding out from Nazis. Nothing to write about. The upsides of a Nazi-free life are more obvious.

One thing our buddy Anne did was to write to Kitty in her diary. Seemed more personal that way, less cheesy than saying "Dear Diary." I doubt you'll ever see this, but somehow writing it to you feels right. We always planned to find our moms together. Maybe once I've done it you'll decide to try it too—then you can use this as a guide.

*Make things easier for you. Seems like that is the least I
could do, after all our years of being friends. Even if you
never do, including you in this project seems like the right
thing. So let's get started!*

*Tip #1: If you want to find your family, start with
figuring out what you already know.*

I closed the book and let out a shaky breath. This would
work. It was going to be better than just working. It was perfect. It was exactly the kind of project that would make the
Duke admissions counselors sit up and take notice. Adopted
girl searches for her birth mom to complete the promise she
made to her former best friend who died too young. It was the
kind of senior project that made people choke up. They'd see
me as more than just a bunch of test scores that weren't quite
up to snuff. Nora had always wanted me to join her on the
great birth-mom quest. Doing this was a way to make it up to
her for blowing her off. It was like finishing her business. Brody
had to agree. I picked up the phone to call him and then put
it back down. It would be harder for him to say no to me face-
to-face. I was going to have to sell him on the idea. I couldn't
let him know how I was sure Duke would like the project, and
how I was willing to do almost anything in order to get in. It
was pretty clear he wasn't that impressed by Duke. He needed
to think I was doing it because it was the right thing and that
it was good for Nora.

I looked at the clock. There was still time before I expected my mom home. No time like the present to get started, and Nora had even given me the first step.

I slid open the hall closet door. I stood on my tiptoes and slipped the scrapbook out from under the odds and ends that had been stacked on top of it, extra lightbulbs and a bulk package of paper towels.

AVERY'S STORY was written on top in raised pink-and-blue plaid letters. You wouldn't think my mom would be crafty. She looked like she would be way more comfortable with a briefcase and law textbooks than with markers or pinking shears, but she could bust out a glue gun like no one else. The scrapbook was mine. It had my name right across the cover, but it still felt a bit like stealing. I stuffed the book under my arm and went back into my room.

The first few pages of the scrapbook had pictures of my parents, looking impossibly young. My dad had a beard that made him resemble a reject from a hippie commune, and my mom had a weird spiky haircut. My mom had drawn thought bubbles coming out of their heads that said things like *Dreaming of Babies* or *New Daddy to Be.*

The next page was dedicated to a giant eight-by-ten baby picture of me. The caption below read *Avery: Two Hours Old.* I looked way older than two hours old. My face was all wrinkled and red. I looked like a six-pound ninety-year-old woman. My head was also strangely cone shaped. No wonder they put a

knitted hat on it; I was practically deformed. I was lucky anyone had wanted me, looking like that. There was also a picture
of my parents holding me. They'd bought me an outfit to come
home in that looked like it was about three sizes too big. My
parents both looked dazed in the picture, as if they couldn't
quite believe someone had just handed them an actual baby.

I flipped to the next page, where there was an envelope
taped down and the caption read *Welcome to the World Letter from Avery's Birth Mom*. I'd read the letter before. I'd been
through the entire scrapbook many times, but I was hesitant to
open it now, in case there might be something new there.

Hello Baby Girl,
I'm afraid of screwing this letter up. It feels like it should
be really important, meaningful. I'm not good at this type
of stuff. Having a baby is the scariest thing I've ever done.
Way scarier than the first time I did a high dive and I
thought I would die. Scarier than any monster or slasher
movie. I'm not sure I've ever been more scared than I
have been the last nine months. And the weird thing is
that I'm still terrified. I thought once you were born it
would be a relief, that it would be over. Now I realize it
isn't over at all, it's the start of something new. You're not
something that happened to me—you're a person. That
kinda freaks me out, and it's also amazing.
The social worker told me to write down what I

*want for you, so here it goes. I hope your life is full of
good things. I wish that you could be safe from stuff like
lies and broken hearts, but I guess that's part of living. I
want you to know that the reason I'm giving you up for
adoption is so that you have the best chance at having a
great life.*

*Right after you were born they let me hold you. I
looked at you and I swear to God you looked back. It was
like you could see into my soul. I know it's pretty much
impossible, but I sort of hope you can remember it. I hope
you turn into a cool person. I am giving you up so you
can have a good life and so I can move on with mine. I
won't be in your life, but I'll never forget you.*

Love,

Lisa

My birth mom was sixteen, almost seventeen, when I was
born. No wonder she'd been unsure of what to say. Her letter
was nice, but it didn't really tell me the things I wanted to know,
like what did she think of my birth dad? Did she ever even consider keeping me? Was she sorry she gave me up? I didn't need a
letter from her; I needed something like a twelve-volume ency-
clopedia set of information.

The scrapbook had copies of the letters my mom had
sent to my birth mom. My adoption had been open, which
meant they had exchanged information, although they never

met face-to-face. My birth mom had picked my parents out of a binder of potential parents, like a catalog of families. The letters my mom sent her after the birth sounded fake and overly cheerful, like those cheesy notes people put in their Christmas cards. *Avery is walking already! She's such a busy little girl who loves her stuffed bunny and music. If the radio is left on, she bops up and down like she's dancing!* There were entirely too many exclamation points. The letters almost sounded like one of those infomercials you see on late night TV. Check out the new and improved Avery! She slices! She dices! She makes egg salad with no mess! Buy one now, and we'll throw in a Chia Pet at no extra cost!!!

I pulled Nora's notebook over and flipped to the back, where there were blank pages. I started to list the things I knew based on the scrapbook, even if I wasn't sure it would be helpful. My birth date, the lawyer who did the adoption, that my birth mom's first name was Lisa.

"What are you doing?"

My head shot up, and my first instinct was to shove the scrapbook under my duvet cover. My mom was standing in the doorway, her suit jacket unbuttoned and her shoes already off and in her hand.

"I didn't hear you come in," I said, stating the obvious. "I was looking through my baby scrapbook."

"What made you pull that old thing out after all this time?" She was trying to act casual, but I could see her hands twisting the ring around her finger.

"Just curious, I guess." I laid my hand on top of the book as if I were swearing a vow. "Why did my birth mom stop writing? She wrote back and forth with you for a couple of years and then nothing." I flipped to the back of the book. By the end my mom hadn't made color-coordinated pages with stickers and captions. Instead a few things were stuffed in the back, including a letter from the adoption organization saying that Lisa no longer wished to do regular updates.

Mom took a deep breath and then came to sit next to me on the bed. "I don't really know for sure. I spoke to our adoption coordinator. She said it isn't uncommon. It can be hard for the birth parent. When Lisa stopped communication, she would have been in college. That can be a difficult time."

"So, she got too busy to bother with me."

"What? No. That's not what I'm saying. I just mean she might have felt that she needed to focus on what was ahead of her instead of the past. By that time she knew how much we loved you. Maybe she could rest a bit easier knowing you had a family. She might have felt that she didn't need to stay involved."

I wondered if she'd made the decision to cut off contact with me because she found it too painful, or because keeping in touch was one more thing on her to-do list and it wasn't worth the hassle.

"What's gotten you interested in all this? Is it what happened with Nora?"

"Sort of." I bit my lower lip. I'd wanted more time to figure out how I was going to tell my parents about my plan. I wanted to have it organized so they'd be impressed, but I ended up spitting it out. "I'm going to make looking for my birth mom my senior project. I'll talk about how I'm doing it to honor what Nora started."

I hadn't expected my mom to leap into the air and declare me a genius, but I also hadn't thought she'd say what she did.

"Absolutely not."

chapter twelve

Tip #2: No matter how much people around you will tell you that adoption is a gift and how the whole process is full of rainbows and unicorns, the truth is it makes people uncomfortable. As soon as you tell people you're looking for your birth mom they'll start telling you why it's a bad idea. What they really mean is they think it's a bad idea. What you think doesn't matter so much to them.

—Field Guide to Finding Your Family

My adoption had never been a secret. It wasn't like my parents sprang the news on me when I was thirteen. I always knew. It wasn't something we talked about very often, but there was a big photo in the hall of me as a baby with them with the saying "Family Is Made, Not Born" on the frame. When some kid teased me about being adopted in second grade, there was a moment when I was pretty sure my dad was going to go all Chuck Norris on his ass.

Along the side of my right hand was a raised scar. I was about seven when I got it. My mom had made her famous lasagna. She took it out of the oven and placed the red ceramic baking dish on a rack on the counter to cool. "Don't touch," she told me. "It's hot!" When she turned away to answer the phone, I reached out and touched the pan. I knew better, but it was somehow irresistible. I can't remember if I thought I would steal a bit of the crusty cheese at the side, or if I just wanted to see how hot it really was, but it was explosively hot. My skin had seared to the side of the dish. I yanked it away, but it was already blistered. Instead of telling my mom, I'd run off to my room and hid. I'd been convinced that if she knew what I had done, they would take me back. I would be in an orphanage with a giant stamp on my file that read TOUCHED HOT DISH AFTER BEING TOLD NOT TO. Who would want a kid who couldn't follow simple directions? If you can't get the hot-dish thing right, it's just a matter of time until you start stealing from the liquor cabinet and taking up recreational drug use. I made myself a vow that I would never give my parents another reason to wish they could give me back. I would be exactly the kid that they had always wanted. I hadn't been perfect, but I'd been as close as I could be. However, my decision to look for my birth mom clearly didn't fit with my mom's idea of her ideal child.

"You can't stop me," I said. We were having a forced family meeting. As soon as my dad had walked in the house, my mom told him about my "scheme" and made us all sit around the kitchen table.

"We certainly can," my mom insisted.

"I'm almost eighteen."

"Almost is not the same as being eighteen." Mom crossed her arms as if that was the end of the argument.

"Are you kidding me?" Our voices were getting louder. My dad's eyes were going back and forth between us like he was watching a tennis game.

Dad held up his hands in surrender. "Can someone tell me why this has come up now? Is there some reason you want to find her?"

"I want to make it my senior project."

Dad cocked his head to the side. "Interesting. The admissions team would like something like that." He winced. Mom had kicked him under the table.

"This isn't about Duke. This is about what's best for Avery. I think dredging all of this up when she's feeling emotionally vulnerable for some silly *school project* isn't a good plan."

Dad nodded. "True."

"This is what I want to do. Both of you are always saying that there's nothing wrong with me being adopted, so why does it matter if I find Lisa?"

"It seems to me that she doesn't want to be found. It was an open adoption. It was her decision to terminate contact." Mom wouldn't meet my eyes.

"But you said yourself that she most likely did that because she was in college. She might want to be in touch now." My frustration levels were growing. I wanted to pound on the table. They'd spent hours helping me brainstorm how to take my application to the next level, and now that I'd found the perfect idea, they weren't going to let me do it.

Mom sighed. "There are a million things you could do your project on. Why don't you pick a women's rights issue? I can help you with all kinds of research."

"Because I want to do this." We stared across the table at each other. "The only reason you don't want me to do this is because you're afraid I'm going to replace you."

She sucked in her breath as if I'd slapped her. I wanted to grab the words out of the air and shove them back into my mouth, but it was too late. She pushed away from the table. "Fine. If that's your decision, by all means look for your birth mom. I wouldn't want to be accused of standing in your way."

"Mom—" I started to say, but she'd already left the room. My dad sat in his chair with an unreadable expression on his face. Ah, just what was missing in my life: more guilt.

"Your mother cares deeply about you. She didn't deserve that."

"I know." I wanted to explain what I was feeling, but I didn't know how.

He got up. "I still haven't had any dinner and it's been a long day. If I were you, I'd make a point to apologize to her." He paused on his way out of the room. "We're not going to stand in your way, but we're also not going to help you with this. It's your project. I hope you know what you're looking for."

"I need to do this, Dad. It's not about you and Mom. It's about me."

"Kiddo, what you don't understand is that if it's about you, it's about all of us."

I slumped against the locker, shocked. "You've got to be kidding me."

Brody slammed his locker shut. "No way. Pick something else. I still think the Aquaman idea rocks, but I'd do education reform before I'd do this."

"My idea rocks. It's not just a topic—it's personal. I'm not saying that Aquaman isn't meaningful, but I'm talking about finding my mom. You have to do this."

Brody shook his head. "No I don't."

The finality in his words annoyed me. How come he'd been willing to do whatever Nora wanted, but didn't even pretend to give my idea any thought?

"Why?" I whined. "It's a good idea, and you've already started doing pictures on the idea of family and finding family, so it's not like you have to repeat anything. It's saving you time."

"Why?" Brody's voice went louder. "Oh, I have no idea. Last time I agreed to do a project with someone to search for her birth mom it went so well. I have no freaking idea why I wouldn't want to do it again." He spun around and marched down the hall.

I trailed after him. "I'm not going to kill myself over this. You don't have to freak out."

"Uh-huh."

"I'm not." I grabbed his sweater, making him stop and turn around. It was time to pull out the big guns. "Look, it's not just about finding my mom. I owe this to Nora. She wanted this for me. This was something she couldn't do, so I need to finish it. Does that make sense?" I made puppy eyes at him.

He closed his eyes. "Yes, but it doesn't change the fact I still think it's a bad idea."

"You and my parents both." Kids streamed past us in the hall, rushing to make their first class. Brody stood there. "It's really important to me. If it wasn't so important, I'd back off," I said.

"Nora told me you didn't care about finding your birth mom," Brody said.

I shifted uncomfortably. Growing up I'd wanted to find my birth mom, but I always knew that my parents wouldn't like the idea. Even though nothing was ever said, I could tell they would be hurt. It felt like saying I didn't think they were doing a good enough job, and there was no way anyone would say they weren't doing a great job in the parenting department. If there was anyone who wasn't up to snuff in our family, it was me. Freshman year I'd mentioned to Shannon and Lydia that I sometimes thought about looking for my birth mom, and they were both confused. Why would I? My parents were perfect. It was the last time I'd mentioned it to anyone until now.

"I'm not sure I can explain it. I realize now that this is something I have to do." I crossed my fingers behind my back. As long as he thought this was about helping me, instead of getting into Duke, he might do it. "I'm not sure I can do it alone. I'm asking for you to help me."

Brody sighed. I could tell my appeal to his desire to be a hero was working.

"So, you'll do it?" I pushed him.

"I don't know."

"I'm going to do it even if you don't help, but I'm asking you to do this with me."

He sighed. "I'll do it."

I squealed and threw myself into his arms, hugging him tightly. He stood there stiff for a moment and then hugged me back. I noticed up close he smelled fresh, like clean air and cedar trees. We both took a step back. I felt awkward and couldn't meet his eyes. "Thank you so much. This means everything," I said.

"Yeah, yeah. It's not like I'm giving you one of my kidneys or something."

"As far as I'm concerned, it's better than a kidney. I won't forget you did it for me." I looked up and smiled at him.

Brody flushed. "I'll do it, but there are going to be rules."

"Rules?"

He yanked on his sweater as if he needed to pull himself together. "Yes, rules. You don't go off and do a bunch of stuff without me. This is a joint project. You include me in whatever you find out."

"Deal." I held out my hand to shake on it.

Brody shook his head. "That was just the first rule. The second rule is if you start having a hard time, you agree that we'll stop."

"I'm not going to have a hard time." I tried to look calm and rational. "Nora and I are different."

"Rule three," Brody said, not commenting on what I'd said. "There's no guarantee we're going to find anyone. We agree now that the project isn't about finding her, but about looking for her. We write it up either way."

"Of course, but I really think we've got a good chance. I have part of a name—"

Brody cut me off. "No obsessing. That's my point."

I crossed my finger over my chest. "No obsessing. Is that it?"

"No. You also agree to go with me for some coffee or something."

I scrunched up my eyebrows. Was he asking me out? "Like a date?"

He flushed. "No, not like a date. So we can sit down and make a plan for the project. I want to know exactly what you're up to."

"No problem. I'll even buy." I wanted to kick myself. I shouldn't have made things awkward. "Is there a rule four?" The warning bell rang, and people in the hall picked up the pace.

"Rule four is that I get to make more rules if I need them."

"Seems a bit unfair. How come you get to make up whatever rules you want?"

Brody smiled. "Because the Aquaman project is still an option." He held out his hand. "Deal?"

I shook his hand. "Deal."

chapter thirteen

This would have been easier if we'd gone for coffee," Brody said.

"But not nearly as tasty."

I've long believed, despite common wisdom, there is no such thing as a bad time for ice cream. If nothing else, because it was so cold outside, we had Melting Moments all to ourselves, which gave me plenty of time to ponder my flavor options.

"I've seen people choose college majors in less time," Brody said.

"Some things can't be rushed." I peered through the freezer case. "I'm torn between my tried-and-true favorite, mint chocolate chip, and vanilla with English toffee bits."

"Get a scoop of both. Otherwise we're still going to be standing here at graduation."

The guy was a genius. "This is a good sign, you know," I said, taking the cup from the clerk. "You've got the kind of problem-solving skills we're going to need for this project."

We grabbed a seat by the window with our ice cream and glasses of water, so that the warm air from the heater blew on our legs. I pulled out a binder and passed him a sheet of paper. "Okay, I made an outline of what the project might look like and broke each bit down into a to-do list." I pointed at the sheet. "I color-coded the items by priority."

Brody looked it over and whistled. "Anyone ever tell you that you're really focused?"

I arched an eyebrow. "Are you calling me anal-retentive? I'll have you know I'm very mellow."

"It's always the mild-mannered ones you have to watch out for. Ever notice after someone goes postal, everyone talks about how normal and quiet they seemed? Can't be a coincidence." Brody used his spoon to steal a bite of my ice cream.

I pretended to be annoyed and pulled my cup out of his reach. "Careful. If you think I can go wild, you've never seen me defend my ice cream. There is no rage like stolen junk food rage."

Brody held up his hands in surrender. He looked back down at the page. "Looks like we've got a place to start, at least. Hopefully the rest of the project comes together this easy." He shifted in his seat. I'd noticed he was almost always in motion. It was like he couldn't be still. As he looked out the window,

I could see there was a small dab of ice cream on his cheek. I reached over with my napkin and wiped it off. He jumped slightly when I touched him.

"Thanks for this," I said.

"You're the one who bought."

Brody had pulled out his wallet, but I'd waved it off and insisted on paying. It seemed like the least I could do. "I didn't mean the ice cream—I meant agreeing to do the project with me. It's going to turn out amazing." I shoved my binder back in my bag. I scraped the bowl. "It's hard to believe we're doing senior projects already. This is a million miles away from the kind of project I thought I'd do."

"I think it's great that you're doing this for Nora instead of picking some topic you think would impress the people at Duke. God, I get so sick of everyone losing their shit about getting into some school just to impress everyone else." He raised his spoon at me. "Not to mention, it is way more interesting than education reform."

A stab of guilt poked me in the chest. Now I was the one shifting in my seat. "It's not wrong to want to get into a good school," I said.

Brody brushed off my comment. "No. It's just that so many people focus on it like it's everything. It's just a college. Four years out of a whole life." He shook his head. "It's moronic."

"But where you go can make a huge difference down the road," I pointed out.

Brody's eyebrows went up. "Down the road? You sound like you're forty. All I'm saying is that people worry too much about where they're going and not enough about what they're doing. Doing the right thing for Nora is what matters. Not selling out to some Ivy League school." He smiled. "I think what you're doing is cool."

Suddenly the ice cream tasted like paste in my mouth. I wanted to explain that I was different. I wanted to get into Duke for the right reasons, but if I admitted now that I was doing the project for the admissions people, he'd hate me.

"Where are you hoping to go next year?" I asked, trying to shift the conversation.

Brody shrugged. "I'm not going to college next year." I almost dropped my spoon, and Brody laughed. "You don't have to look that shocked. I'm taking a year off, not planning to join the circus."

He seemed so calm and sure about it, as if he didn't have any doubt it was the right plan. "Aren't you worried that you'll get behind?" I asked.

"Behind what? Life's a marathon, not a sprint. I feel like I need a year to figure out what I want."

"So what are you going to do?" My mind started to turn through the options. "You could talk to some of the local photographers. They might take you on like an apprentice."

Brody chuckled. "The world is a lot bigger than Lansing. My plan right now is to spend a couple of months after graduation bumming around Europe taking pictures. When the money runs out, I'm going to go to New York. I've got a cousin living in Brooklyn who will let me crash on his couch for a couple months while I try and get a job."

I knew there were people who did things like this, but it seemed like something you'd read in a book. Everyone I knew was going to college. A big school if they could, and if not, then one of the local community colleges. There was a girl in our class who was going into the army, but that was about as exotic as anyone got. "Wow."

"I don't know if it's that exciting. It feels like high school has been this holding pattern. I want to get out. Do stuff."

"Are you scared?" I blushed. Now he was going to think I was some kind of coward.

"Hell yeah. Are you kidding? I'm totally freaked out. With my luck I'll fall into a Paris sewer or something. I don't exactly have the best coordination." He finished off his ice cream and tossed his cup into the trash. It hit the rim and then fell to the floor.

"Trying to prove your point?" I asked.

He leaned over and picked up the cup and dumped it in the trash. "Apparently." He rubbed his hands on his pants. "Sorry if I got down on where you want to go to school. I'm sure Duke's great."

"It is," I said.

"I'm just glad it's not the focus of your life." Brody's spoon dove back into my ice cream, stealing another bite. "That's pathetic when people get like that. So, what do you want to do?"

"Like a major?"

"No, what do you want to do in life?"

I realized I was shredding the napkin and forced myself to put it down on the table. "It's not that easy."

Brody barked out a laugh. "Are you kidding? It's just about the hardest thing in the world." He reached across the table and took my hands. "Close your eyes," he ordered me.

"What?" I looked around to see if the ice-cream clerk was paying attention to us.

"Close 'em."

I closed my eyes. His hands were warm, his thumb ran over the backs of my fingers, and I felt my breath catch.

"Okay, now list things that make you happy. No order. Doesn't matter if they're stupid or random, just list things that make you happy."

I opened my eyes. "What's the point of this?"

"The point is to figure out where to start. Try again. Close your eyes and tell me what makes you happy."

I closed my eyes and my mind was blank. I couldn't think of a thing that made me happy except for the fact that he was holding my hand, but you could stick a spoon in my eyes before I was going to admit that. "I don't know," I said.

"Don't give up. Just think about what kinds of things make you happy."

"Office supplies," I spit out. My eyes flew open. "That sounds stupid. I don't know why I said that."

"No it doesn't. Close 'em again. You like new notebooks, Post-it Notes . . ." His voice trailed off, waiting for me to fill in the next word.

"I like how expensive paper feels. And pens. I like those Sharpie markers that come in different colors." Things started to rush into my head. "I like the sound of waves on a beach and how clothes that dried outside in the sun smell. I like really salty popcorn, being inside during a thunderstorm, and wrapping presents. I like writing and telling stories, and the feel of dogs' ears, how they're sort of soft and silky." My eyes opened again; did I actually just admit a love for rubbing dog ears? Brody was smiling. I pulled my hands back and took a drink of my water, the straw making a sucking sound as it pulled in the last of the water from around the crushed ice. "I guess it's clear: After graduation I need to move to the beach and get a dog."

"It's a place to start." Brody stood and gathered up our napkins. "You don't have to know the destination, just where to begin. Starting with what makes you happy is never a bad place."

"While the dog and beach plan has merit, I feel like what I need to do first is find my birth mom and get through the rest of senior year." I pushed away the rest of my ice cream and stood so I could stretch.

"You know she's not going to have all the answers."

"She doesn't need to have them all. It's just a place to make a start."

Brody laughed. "Now you're stealing my best lines."

"Why would I steal the crappy ones?"

Brody threw his arm around me. "Excellent point."

I leaned into his side; the warm weight of his arm on my shoulders felt good. I glanced up, and standing outside the window, Shannon and Lydia were looking in, their mouths open.

chapter fourteen

If there were awards for being persistent, then my friend Shannon would win one. There are people preparing for the Olympics or a moon landing who are less focused than her. As soon as we sat down with our trays in the cafeteria, she started back in again.

"It's no big deal. I just didn't know you guys were hanging out."

"You knew Brody and I became partners for our senior project," I said.

"It didn't look like you guys were working on homework," Shannon said under her breath.

"What did you guys decide to do as your project?" Lydia asked.

For some reason I didn't want to tell them. It wasn't that I didn't think they'd be supportive, but it seemed like something I wanted to keep between Brody and me. "We're doing something on different family structures. Like how families should be defined."

Shannon picked at her salad. Her fork chased a cherry tomato around the plate, trying to spear it.

"What's the big deal, anyway? Brody's nice," I said. Shannon and Lydia exchanged a glance. I tossed my fork down on my tray. "Okay, seriously, guys, stop doing that. It makes me feel like you're talking about me all the time."

Lydia's face scrunched up in an expression of concern. She'd make a great kindergarten teacher someday. "We're not talking about you in a bad way. We're worried about you."

"Why? I'm fine."

Shannon sniffed. "I wouldn't call it fine." She started ticking items off on her fingers before I could argue. "Nora died, your early app for Duke was shot down, you and Colton busted up, you haven't made it to cheer practice in weeks, and now you're spending all your time with Brody, who's weird."

"He's not weird," I protested.

"He's weird," Shannon said. She held up a hand to cut me off. "Don't get me wrong, I'm not saying he's a freak or something, but he doesn't fit in with anyone. He wanders around the halls with that camera like he's from another planet—"

Lydia cut her off. "I'm sure he's nice. It's more that he's not part of our crowd." She looked over her shoulder to see if anyone was paying attention to our conversation and leaned forward so she could drop her voice. "Don't tell Karl I told you, but Colton is totally bummed you guys broke up. He told Karl that he thought he made a mistake by letting you get away. Being sorta cool and hard to get is a good thing, but if Colton thought you'd hooked up with someone else, he'd never get in the middle of something like that."

"I'm not sure I want to get back together with Colton," I said.

"Now, see, that's weird. Brody's weirdness is rubbing off on you." Shannon pointed at me with her fork. "Colton's hot, he's popular, and just about any girl in this school would kill to go out with him."

I had an image of hordes of teen girls going all Hunger Games in a death match to win Colton's hand.

"He'd never break your heart again," Lydia said. "The way Karl talks, he's really upset."

I wondered when Colton started sharing his deep feelings with Karl. Or when he started having all these deep feelings for me at all, for that matter. If Colton hadn't really been in love with me when we went out, I had a hard time believing he was now suddenly completely head over heels. This whole thing was most likely Lydia's fantasy. She liked when we dated friends. It made things so easy. My best guess was that Colton, if he'd said anything at all, told Karl that he thought I was okay. Or that he missed making out. It wasn't so much me as a ready access to boobs.

"Fine, skip Colton for a minute. What about cheer?" Shannon said. "We've been practicing with Liz, but she's nowhere near as good as you. When are you coming back?"

I'd continued to make excuses to Coach Kerr about going to cheer practice, and for the time being she was giving me space. Having a friend, even a friend you hadn't really hung out with in years, kill herself meant you got a lot of space. My history teacher had even told me I didn't need to do my presentation on American heroes, and it might be my imagination, but I was pretty sure the cafeteria lady was giving me extra applesauce when she dished things out.

"I don't know when I'll be back," I said.

"The basketball team counts on us. They start their games next week," Shannon said.

I rolled my eyes. "Our team sucks. The fact we're standing there yelling out chants doesn't make any difference."

Shannon pulled back as if I'd suddenly pushed down a saint. "Wow. I guess I had no idea you thought what we did was so stupid."

"That's not what she means," Lydia said, trying to smooth things over. "She's just not feeling like herself." She turned to me. "Right?"

I sighed. I didn't know how to explain that I wasn't even sure what feeling like myself would be like. I didn't have a clue who I was anymore. "It isn't that I think cheer is stupid. It's that I'm not feeling like it's something I want to do right now."

"So can we agree that you're not fine?" Shannon made finger quotes in the air when she said "fine."

The girl was level-five persistent. "Okay, you win. I'm not fine, but there's nothing wrong with me either. I just need some time. Everything in my life turned upside down, and I need to get my feet back under me. I need to know you guys have my back."

Lydia raised her can of Diet Coke. "Always." Shannon raised her water bottle and waited for me to raise mine. We clicked over the table, sealing the deal.

"So now that we have that out of the way, what is the deal with Brody? Do you like him?" Shannon asked, popping a hunk of cucumber in her mouth. "I'm telling you, we saw you guys through the window and the sparks were flying."

"There were no sparks," I said. "We were just celebrating getting started on our project. C'mon, you guys know me, do I ever turn down an opportunity for ice cream?" I shifted uncomfortably in my seat. I didn't want to talk about him. It was like what was happening with Brody was completely separate from the rest of my life, and I didn't like the two parts mixing together. Shannon and Lydia were great, but anytime any of us had a crush or started dating anyone, the whole situation had to be dissected and explored. We practically busted out a whiteboard so the whole thing could be diagrammed with colored markers. I wanted to keep Brody to myself. "I'd go with anyone if they offered ice cream. It doesn't mean anything."

Shannon snorted. "Sparks, fireworks. I'm telling you there was a boom. Fever. Heat." She licked her finger and made a sizzling sound.

"I don't like Brody, okay? We're just friends. We're not even really that—we're just partners for this stupid project."

Lydia's mouth opened into a perfect circle and her eyes were wide. *Shit.* I turned around slowly and saw Brody standing right behind me. The words in my mouth dried up.

"Hey," I croaked.

"I wanted to give you this." Brody passed me a manila envelope. "It's the pictures I'd already taken for the project."

"Oh. Thanks." An awkward silence fell over the table.

"I didn't know you took pictures. That's so cool," Lydia said in an overly perky voice.

Brody stared at her without answering and then looked back at me. "See you around." He turned and wove through the crowd in the cafeteria. He pushed his way through the large group hanging out near the door and walked out. I wanted to jump up and follow him, but I was pretty sure he didn't want to talk to me, and even if I caught up with him, I had no idea what I'd say. Lately I didn't seem capable of talking to anyone without screwing it up.

"See what I mean? The guy is weird," Shannon said.

I went to the Human Services office after school. When we'd planned it, Brody had said he'd come with me, but I didn't see him the rest of the day. I hung around his locker after classes, but he didn't show up. I sent him a text, but he didn't text me back. There was no denying it: Either aliens had kidnapped him, or he was avoiding me. I decided to go ahead without him. Maybe I'd find out something and have an excuse to contact him again. I knew he'd want to hear what happened.

My heart was slamming in my chest. My skin felt hyper-aware and itchy. I couldn't remember the last time I felt this nervous. I made myself take three deep breaths, exhaling slowly. I'd thought about calling, maybe calling from a pay phone at the mall like it was a bomb threat that I didn't want traced to my home phone, but I knew that was a stupid idea. All I was asking for was some information. Going in person was still the best plan.

I yanked open the door to the Department of Human Services and stepped inside. It looked like every other government office I'd ever been in: industrial furniture, informational posters taped to the wall, and worn carpet on the floor. There was a group of people milling around the lobby, and at the front a few desks behind a counter. I walked up to one of them.

"Excuse me," I started.

The woman didn't even look up from what she was doing and instead pointed to the far wall. I turned but didn't see anything.

"I was hoping—" I got out before she cut me off.

"Take a number." Her finger pointed again at the back

wall, and this time I saw one of those number-slip dispensers like they had at the deli.

I slunk across the room. I could feel the eyes of everyone else in the room watching me, the one person who didn't know how things worked. I pulled a number and took a seat. The woman next to me was holding a baby whose entire upper lip was coated in snot. I inched over as far as I could to avoid the baby's grasping hands. The kid was a little carrier of plague.

The ticking of the clock on the wall seemed to slow down. I should have brought something to do. I crossed my legs and jostled my foot until the woman next to me raised her eyebrow in annoyance. "Sorry," I whispered. I picked up some of the pamphlets on the table. Everything I ever wanted to know about food stamps and job programs. I was almost ready to walk out when someone finally called my number.

I went up to the desk. My voice caught in my throat for a second. "I'm looking for some information about an adoption." The woman's fingers flew over the keyboard, her computer full of the information I needed. "How does an individual go about requesting information about their birth parents?" My face was flushed red hot, but my voice was coming out even and calm.

"The record can be requested through CAR."

"Car?" I scrambled to find a pen in my purse to write this down. She pushed a pen hooked on a chain over to me.

"Central Adoption Registry. The individual can also go directly to the agency or attorney that handled the adoption.

Do you know if the person was born before or after September 1980?"

"After," I said.

"Great, that makes things a bit easier. The rules changed after that. The adoptee fills out the CAR clearance form, FIA 1921. Assuming the birth parent hasn't requested a denial statement, the adoptee will be forwarded a copy of their original birth certificate."

I made notes as she talked. I'd have to hope that my birth mom never got around to filing any formal paperwork saying she didn't want to be in touch. I could picture all too easily my request form with a giant "DENIED" stamped across the top in red. "How do I get one of these clearance forms? Do you have them here?"

"So is this for you?"

"Yes." I tried to stand straighter. It felt like she was looking at me differently, searching for a defect. As if she was trying to figure out why someone would give me away.

"Are you over eighteen?"

I thought about lying, but then realized that she was likely going to ask for some kind of identification. "No."

She paused for a beat. "Under Michigan law you can't request information about your adoption until you're eighteen. Your adoptive family can make the request on your behalf if you want it sooner than that."

"But it's my adoption."

"I understand, but the law requires you to be eighteen. Even if you go directly to the agency, they'll require you to meet the age requirement."

My jaw tightened. "That's not fair. I'm not asking for information about someone else, I'm asking for basic information about me. I'm asking for my mom's name, not military secrets. I bet you know the name of your mom."

"I understand it must be frustrating." She wasn't even looking at me anymore. I could see that she had her e-mail open on her computer screen. All I was now was someone keeping her from more interesting things.

I felt like screaming that she had no idea how frustrating or she wouldn't keep answering in that quiet, measured tone, like she was telling me the weather instead of denying me what I had a right to know.

"I'm seventeen," I explained. "I'll be eighteen in May. I'm not nine. We're talking about the difference of a couple of months."

"Then you can request the forms in a few months. I'm afraid before then I can't assist you."

"You mean you *won't* help me." I knew I sounded like a whiny toddler, but since my maturity didn't matter, only my specific birth date, I didn't see the point of pretending to be grown-up on the issue. There was no use explaining that in a couple of months Duke will have already made their decision and it would be too late.

"Would you like the number of a social worker in your area? Maybe someone you can talk to?" She reached behind her to pull a brochure off of a stack.

"There's nothing wrong with me. I don't need to talk to someone, I need someone to give me the information I should be entitled to."

She sighed. "Then I suggest you come back after your birthday."

I whirled around and stomped off before she could tell me to have a nice day. I could hear the beep, and they called the next number. I wanted some answers. Now I just had to figure out how to get them.

chapter fifteen

I sent Brody two more texts, but he didn't respond. I found myself lurking in the hall near his locker over the next two days so that I might casually run into him, but I didn't. I'd looked through the pictures he'd given me in the cafeteria. They were amazing. They weren't pictures like I would take. They looked like the kind of photos you saw hanging in art galleries. There was something about them, something that made me feel there was so much more happening outside of the frame. There was one of a dad pushing his little girl in a swing. Her mouth was caught mid-laugh as she rushed forward. The dad looked proud, but also vaguely left behind. I'd look at it and start wondering about what the people in the picture were thinking. Now I understood the saying that a picture is worth a thousand words. His pictures were stories.

My favorite was a black-and-white photograph of a little girl in a dress. She was sitting on a fallen log at the edge of a dark forest. It seemed as if beyond where the light reached, there might be a wolf, or a wicked witch with a poisoned apple. I'd propped the photo up on my nightstand so it was the first thing I saw every morning when I woke up. I found it disturbing, but at the same time I couldn't stop looking at it. I hadn't done anything else on the project. I wasn't sure what my next steps should be, and I had the sinking feeling that Brody didn't want to do the project with me anymore. My stupid comments in the cafeteria had ruined everything. Friday afternoon I'd slipped a Batman sticker through the vent on his locker. I didn't know what else to do.

I knew my parents were surprised I was home with them on a Friday night, but we were pretending it was normal. I sat curled up in a chair. My parents were on the sofa while we all watched a horror movie my dad had downloaded. There had been a big group of my friends going to the movies, but I didn't want to go. Colton would be there. Lydia and Shannon had tried to convince me that this would be perfect, a no-stress chance to hang out again. A non-date date. I could picture the two of them manipulating things so that Colton and I would be sitting next to each other in the theater. Lydia would keep talking about all the great times we had when we were together, trying to remind him. I knew Colton would press his leg to mine, and then sometime in the middle of the movie he would reach over and take my hand. And then what would I do? Hold his back? That would be the easy thing. Everyone in our group liked when Colton and I were going out. It made things tidier. Evened up the numbers. Made sure no one felt awkward. Since I didn't know how to handle it, I'd pleaded that I was coming down with something and bailed on my friends. Not that there was anything wrong with hanging with my parents in comfy sweats and eating my mom's famous butter-and-parmesan-cheese popcorn, but it felt a bit like hiding out.

My dad jumped when the doorbell rang. He acted tough, but scary movies freaked him out.

"I got it," I offered, unfolding myself from the chair, tossing off the afghan. I glanced at myself in the mirror above the hall table. I hoped my friends hadn't decided to stop by to kidnap me on the way to the movies. I didn't have any makeup on and my hair was tied back with an elastic. I looked bad enough they might believe my lie about being sick.

"Careful, it might be the undead," Dad called out. My mom punched him in the shoulder. "Brains . . . ," he moaned.

I opened the door. Brody was standing there, his lower face hidden by a scarf. I stood there blinking at him.

"Surprise." His breath came out like white smoke.

I took a step back into the house to make space. "Do you want to come in?"

Brody shook his head. "Nah. Can you come out?"

"Now?"

"Well, you could come out later, but I wouldn't be here. It's sort of cold to wait around."

I blinked and then poked my head into the living room. "Do you mind if I go out for a bit?"

My parents' heads swiveled in tandem to check out the clock above the fireplace. "It's getting late," Mom said.

"A friend of mine is outside. We're going to take a walk."

"Friend?" Dad asked in that voice that implied he was considering having Brody come in and fill out a biography form and complete a full psychological workup.

"His name is Brody." I crossed my fingers that they wouldn't make him come in and do the whole "so tell us about yourself" thing. "He's the one I'm doing my senior project with."

Mom started to shake her head, but Dad's hand reached over and took hers. "You be back in an hour," he said.

Mom turned to argue with him, but there must have been something in his expression that changed her mind. "Take your mittens. It's cold."

"I will." I bolted for the hall closet and pulled out my jacket.

"And a scarf. It's really cold out there."

I stepped outside, my breath freezing in my lungs. "I'm glad you came over," I said.

"Sure." He didn't look at me. "I would have called you back, but I was really busy this week."

"No problem." I knew he was lying, but it didn't seem like the time to argue. "I'm glad you're here now."

He pulled the Batman sticker out of his jacket pocket. "You sent me the Bat-Signal, so I knew I had to respond."

My parents were standing by the living room window, looking out at us. I pulled him toward the street. "Let's take a walk."

"Or we could give them something to watch. I could start doing some interpretive dance." Brody started to jerk around.

I giggled. I grabbed his arm and steered him down the sidewalk. "What are you doing here?"

"I thought we should talk and figure out what we're doing."

My face flushed, and I was glad the scarf covered it. "I'm happy the bat signal worked."

"It's my dance moves, isn't it? Chicks dig guys who can dance." Brody busted out another funky move that made him look like a squirrel that had accidentally bitten into an electrical wire. He stopped dancing. "It's good you were home. I thought you might be out."

"A bunch of people went to the movies, but I didn't feel like it."

"I heard you and Colton were getting back together." His hands were shoved deep in his pockets.

"No." I shuffled through the last of the fall leaves that hadn't been raked up. "It's complicated. Everyone in our group sort of wants us to get back together, and it wasn't like there was some big reason we broke up. Colton's not a bad guy. I just don't think he's the guy for me. It's like we don't fit."

He looked down the street as if he were fascinated by the Christmas decorations some of the neighbors had already put up. "I thought that might be why you blew me off." He shrugged like it was no big deal. "You know, you didn't need to worry. No one would think you'd choose me over Colton. King of the senior class."

"I'm so sorry about what I said in the cafeteria. I didn't mean it to sound how it came out." I realized I was biting my lip and made myself stop. I wanted to tell him that he was way more interesting than Colton, but that seemed the wrong thing to say.

"I came by to say if you don't want to be partners for this project, it's fine with me. Bradshaw kinda shoved us together. If you'd rather do something with your friends, it's okay."

"I don't," I said. "I want to do this with you." I grabbed the sleeve of his coat to make him stop. I had to convince him. "Please do this project with me. I don't think I could do it without you."

chapter sixteen

I held my breath, waiting to see if he was still willing to do the project. It wasn't that I couldn't do it on my own, but I didn't want to anymore.

"Okay." He paused as we walked up to the park at the entrance to my subdivision. He crunched through the leaves to the swing set. He bent gallantly down and motioned that I should take the first swing. He sat next to me and pushed off, his legs pumping so that his swing started to reach for the sky. "What did you find out when you went to the state office?"

I felt the tension in my stomach disappear. For a second I'd been afraid he'd walk away and leave me standing there. "Not much. Unless I'm willing to wait until I'm eighteen, they won't tell me anything."

"Not too surprising. Nora didn't have any luck that way

either. We should go to the library. There's a bunch of research Nora and I did when we were looking for her mom. Some of it might help us."

I leaned back so that I was looking up at the sky. "I was thinking about Nora today. We're coming up to the first of the firsts. Next week will be the first Thanksgiving Nora won't be around. Then there will be the first Christmas she won't be here, the first New Year, the first summer vacation, the first start of school, and the first anniversary of her death. Then eventually it will be the second of everything, and then after that I'll have to think about how long it's been since she was alive, take time to calculate it." I watched the stars slide past as I swung back and forth.

"You won't forget her—that's what matters, not if you can say how many years or weeks since she's been gone." In the cold air his breath plumed out like dragon smoke from his mouth.

"What if I do? What if I get to a point where it seems easier to not think about her? What if a few years from now she doesn't even cross my mind, and my life goes on like I never even knew her?"

Brody raised his eyebrows. "What makes you think that will happen?"

"People do. They move on. Everyone is always talking about how we'll all be friends forever, but you know we won't. Everyone will go off. Some people will stay in touch, but not most of us. After graduation there will be a time when we won't remember everyone's names anymore without being prompted."

"Forgetting large chunks of high school might be a good thing. Sort of a way of dealing with PTSD."

"It's not just school. My birth mom moved on. She decided she didn't want to be bothered anymore, and I was her child. She used to keep in touch with my mom, and then when I was about four, she stopped. Maybe she got sick of celebrating the first, second, third, fourth Christmas we were apart, the fourth birthday and so on. Maybe it wasn't worth it anymore, easier to forget."

"Could be," Brody acknowledged. "I don't know your birth mom. It's possible that she couldn't be bothered with having a kid anymore. There's no real way to know."

"Can you just accept that? That there's no reason?"

He pumped the swing back and forth. "Lots of stuff in life doesn't have a good reason. My dad left a few years ago. I wanted there to be a reason. That he was seeing someone else, or that my mom spent all his money, or even that I was such a disappointment to him that he couldn't stand it anymore. But nope. Nothing. He got sick of being married and being a dad."

"Do you see him anymore?"

Brody sighed. "Sort of. It's this thing where I feel like he sees me because his parents, my grandparents, guilt him into it. Last year my mom moved us here so she could be closer to her sister. He hasn't been great with making his child support and she wanted more help. My dad lives back in Oregon. He acted like he was bummed that we wouldn't get together much, but I think he's relieved. It's like the perfect excuse." He mimicked his dad's voice. "Gosh, son, I'd love to see you, but darn it all, you're halfway across the country. Maybe some other time."

My feet traced the groove under the swing. "That sucks."

"Yeah. Not much I can do about it. It's his call. All sorts of people in the world, some good, some bad. Sometimes there are good people who do bad things. The issue isn't what your birth mom would do or wouldn't do. It's about you. You aren't the type to forget Nora. That's what matters."

The night air was cold, but I didn't want to go home. "What if I'm like Lisa? What if I walk away from people when things get difficult? I basically walked away from Nora when she was alive. I didn't completely dump her as a friend, but I certainly didn't go out of my way, either."

Brody stopped his swing, his foot dragging in the wood chips. "Is this one of those things where you ask if you look fat in an outfit just so I'll tell you that no, you look amazing?"

"No," I insisted.

"Everyone makes mistakes. My dad should try harder. I'm his kid. Maybe you should have made more time for Nora. Maybe your birth mom made a mistake when she stopped the letters. But that's not the point. Being a good person isn't just about what you've done."

I forced myself to stop staring up into the sky. It was making me dizzy, like I might suddenly fly free of the swing and disappear into the darkness. "If it isn't about what you've done, what is it about?"

"About what you choose to do next."

I realized Brody was staring at me. I spun my swing so we were knee to knee. I could feel the heat of his body through the fabric of his jeans. His knee was pressed against mine. A shock ran up my back at the touch. I leaned forward slightly and so did he. His breath was warm on my face. "You're a good person," I said quietly.

He stood up suddenly so he was standing on the swing. I blinked. I'd been so sure he was about to kiss me. The night air froze the warm space where his breath had warmed my skin.

"You should stand up here too."

I slid my hands along the metal links of the chains and pulled myself up, swinging slightly off balance. The height made everything look different. The two of us looked out across the park. I could see my house. My parents had all the lights on, so that pools of warm light were reaching out into the night. I knew they would wait up until I got home.

"Have you thought about what you'll do next?" Brody asked.

I thought about answering that I'd thought I would kiss him, but I didn't have nearly the guts to put the words out there. "About what?" I asked instead.

"How will you handle it if you find her?"

His comment surprised me. My foot slipped off the swing

and I had to catch myself before I fell. "I don't know. I have this image where we get to be almost like friends. It's not like I want her to be my mom or suddenly where we're besties. It's just I'd like to know her. I want her to want to know me. I have all these questions I'd like to ask."

"How do your parents feel about all of this? Any better?"

I blew a long breath out. "Not good. They say they get it, that they understand, but I know they wish I'd leave it alone. We're pretending the whole thing isn't happening. They don't ask about it and I don't talk. It's funny in a way. I think my mom worries that I want to find my birth mom because there's something she didn't do right, but that's not it. My parents are—" My brain scrambled to find the word. "Perfect. My mom is a lawyer who still found time to hand sew each of my Halloween costumes, and my dad was the kind who hung on to the back of my bike and ran alongside for blocks while I learned to ride."

"I'm trying to understand the part where having perfect parents is a bad thing."

I laughed. "It's more that I've always felt like I didn't quite match up to what they wanted. That they should have gotten this perfect kid, someone to keep up the standards. It's like if I can find my birth mom, I'll know where I come from, maybe make sense of it. I don't know how to explain it." There were also things I couldn't explain, to him or my parents. If I didn't get into Duke, then everything I'd done so far was for nothing.

Now that I'd started the project, it wasn't just about getting into Duke anymore. There were so many things I wanted to ask Lisa that weren't in any of the paperwork from the adoption agency that my parents had saved in my scrapbook. I had a medical history and a letter, but they'd left so much out. My freakishly long second toe, did she have that too? When she was angry or anxious, did she break out in blotchy red-hot hives all over her chest? How did she know she was in love with my birth dad? Had she loved him? Most importantly, did she still think about me, or was she glad I was gone?

"Hate to break it to you, but feeling like you're letting your parents down is sort of universal, even if you share the same genetic material." Brody jumped down from the swing so that he was standing on the ground. He offered his hand to help me down. I stepped onto the ground next to him. "You should prepare yourself for that, for when we find her."

"You really think we'll find her?"

"Yeah. I do."

"Oh my God. I'm going to do this." My heart started to race. I'd been so focused on impressing Duke that I hadn't thought past that moment. If the project went well, I would meet my birth mom. It was as if I'd stumbled and suddenly realized I was standing on the edge of the Grand Canyon. I almost couldn't breathe. "I'm going to find her. We're going to find her."

Brody nodded. "That was kinda the point."

I threw myself into his arms with a whoop. He held me for a second, but the shift in weight threw him off balance. Brody slipped on the leaves underfoot, and we fell backward into a pile of wood chips. He let out a loud *ooph* as I landed on top of him.

"Shit. Are you okay?" I pulled myself up on my elbow.

"You might consider giving a guy some warning before you use your ninja moves on him."

I started giggling. "I thought you were Batman. Aren't you supposed to have lightning-fast reflexes?"

He propped himself up and smiled, then tossed a handful of frozen leaves into my face. I sucked in a breath in shock and then spit out a piece of leaf. Brody laughed, so I reached over and shoved a handful of leaves down the neck of his coat.

He held his hands in the air. "Truce." He pointed up at the sky. "Check it out—shooting star."

I looked up and saw a streak of light.

"Make a wish," Brody said. He closed his eyes, and I knew he was wishing for something. I felt an ache. What I would have wished for was that he felt comfortable telling me his wishes and that I could tell him everything.

chapter seventeen

My brain felt ready to explode. I pushed away the book I was reading. Or pretending to read. My brain was full and I couldn't fit in another single thing. The huge Thanksgiving dinner my mom had made two days ago might still be blunting my thoughts. Too many carbs. We couldn't do anything on the Friday because everything except the mall was closed, but Brody had picked me up first thing this morning to go to the library. I stretched and my neck made a cracking sound. We'd been here for hours. The past few pages the words had started to blur together as I tried to read. Brody was still working away on his laptop. Every so often he'd write something down and then go back to searching. He seemed to sense I was staring and looked over.

"Any luck?" he whispered. We were in a corner of the

library. We'd pushed two of the study carrels together so we could work on the project. It was sunny outside, which meant the library was nearly empty. It felt like we were the only people there.

"Not really. I made some notes about adoption law so we have some general research for the presentation. The whole system seems sort of screwed up to me. Everything varies from state to state and depends on when you were adopted. The rules keep changing." I flipped the book I'd been looking through closed. "Based on the call I made last week to the adoption lawyer my parents used, we're not going to get any info from them, either." This was an understatement. I hadn't been able to get past the secretary. Without my parents' okay, they weren't going to tell me a thing. They wouldn't even confirm they'd handled the adoption.

"Don't worry about it. We'll find another way." Brody pushed over the list he'd been working on. "Here's every online site I can find on adoptees seeking info on birth parents. I went through and registered you on the sites with your birth date, her first name, and the hospital where you were born. If your birth mom is looking for you, the system will match you up."

"Seems like if she was looking, she could contact the adoption agency."

Brody shook his head. "In theory, but you never know. Maybe your parents didn't update your address. You said you guys moved when you were in seventh grade, so maybe she can't find you through them. Or it's possible she contacted them and they told her too much time had passed since she terminated contact. There might be some kind of rule about that. Maybe she thinks she doesn't want to bother you if you don't want to be bothered. If she did it this way, she might figure no one will bug you unless you want to be found."

I felt a flicker of hope in my chest. "Do you really think that's possible?"

"Anything's possible."

"It's weird to think that there could be an e-mail that just pops up, and suddenly I'm in touch with her." I tried to imagine what that would feel like to see her name and address on my screen. I had the urge to check my phone in case she'd already sent a message.

"Promise me if someone contacts you that you'll talk to me first before trying to meet up." Brody's voice was serious.

"In case she's a con artist."

"Like I said, anything's possible." Brody twisted his head from side to side to get the kink out of his neck.

"What if she doesn't contact me?" I tapped my pen on the book in front of me.

"We'll give this a week, and if we don't hear anything, then we'll try a different way. We have some info on Lisa. There has to be a way to find her. It's not like she's in the witness protection program or anything." He stretched his legs out. I wanted to put a finger in the hole in his jeans just above his knee. He was tall enough that his feet almost reached the far shelf of books. "Presentations aren't due until January, when school's back in session. That gives us plenty of time."

"A month." I could have told him the exact number of days and hours, but didn't want to come across as obsessed.

"Since we started late, we could ask Bradshaw to let us go last. That pushes us into February."

There was no way to tell him the problem was that I needed to find my birth mom in time to add the presentation to my Duke application. I didn't have until February. "I don't want to push it back. I'd rather get it done."

"You're always in a rush," Brody said. "Enjoy the process."

"Maybe." I smiled at him and shifted the conversation. "You know what I am enjoying? Your photos. They're amazing."

He blushed. "I'll take more over the next couple of weeks. I'm trying to get all different kinds of shots that show family."

"Have you thought about going to art school?"

"I don't like the idea of people sitting around judging them." He shrugged. "I'm not sure I'm up for the rejection."

"Look at it this way: You're already not in art school. Worst thing that would happen if you applied and they rejected you is that you still wouldn't be in." I reached over to squeeze his arm. "I'm not being nice. I'm serious. They're really good."

Brody stared down at his sneakers as if they were suddenly going to give him the secret of life. "Maybe."

"How can you not know they're good? People must tell you all the time."

"You and Nora are the only ones who have seen them." He shifted in his seat, his feet tapping on the floor. "Nora convinced me this project was the excuse I needed to show some off. You know how she could be."

"Your parents haven't seen them?" I tried to imagine it. If I'd shown even the slightest interest in taking pictures, my parents would have gone out and bought me a camera with a zoom lens capable of taking shots of the moon, made sure I was signed up to take classes with the next Ansel Adams, and had a full framed gallery of all my pictures down the hallway.

"My dad still has me frozen at thirteen. He asks me about sci-fi movies that I liked back then. He doesn't have a clue what I'm interested in now. My mom—" Brody paused. "It's like she's mad all the time. Mad my dad left. Mad she's stuck having to go back to nursing and working shifts at the hospital. Mad she felt like she had to move back here and live with her sister. Most of the time I try and fly under her radar."

"Well, I think your pictures are amazing, and if your parents don't see it, then they're blind."

"Parents don't see their own kids. At least not clearly." Brody closed his laptop. "I don't know, maybe it gets easier when you move out."

"At least there's hope," I said, trying to lighten the mood.

"Always." He smiled. "So which picture was your favorite?"

I pulled my knees up onto the chair and wrapped my arms around them while I thought about it. "Hmm. I liked them all, but my favorite was the picture of the little girl by the woods. What's its story?"

"What do you think it is?"

I should have known he wouldn't give me the answer easily. I pulled our project folder out of my bag and shook the pictures out of the envelope onto the table. I picked through to find the photo. I liked it as much as I had before. I held it out at arm's length. "It seems a bit ominous to me. Like something in that wood is about to eat her."

Brody turned his head as if he wanted a different view of the photograph. "The truth is less dangerous. I was at a park. There was a kid's birthday party going on. Her mom had organized some type of game, and the birthday girl wanted nothing to do with it. Her mom told her if she didn't want to play nice with everyone, then she could be by herself. She stomped off and sat down. That's when I took the shot. I thought it was sort of showing the isolation you feel sometimes. It's like your parents throw you a party, and it's still a bummer. I liked it. I thought it looked sort of fairy tale–like. Different perspective, I guess."

I laughed. "Guess I got carried away reading something into that one. I thought fairy tales were supposed to be all pretty princesses, singing mice, and happily-ever-afters. She looks seriously unhappy."

"Not true on the singing mice. Read the original Grimm's fairy tales. They're some pretty dark stuff. Besides, there's no wrong thing to see in a picture. Pictures are like crystal balls. Different people see different things."

"What does what I saw say about me?"

"That you feel stalked by monsters."

chapter eighteen

I'd been waylaid on the way to the bathroom. My best guess was that she'd been waiting for me and pounced when she saw me alone.

"Ms. Scott!"

I froze in place. "Hey, Coach." I should have known there was only so long I could avoid her. I knew she likely had regretted giving me time off ten minutes after she agreed to it.

"You know, I was happy to give you a break from things, a chance to get your feet under you after what happened."

I knew this talk was coming. Grief was one thing, but it was starting to mess with Coach Kerr's cheer program. "I appreciate it."

"You know what I say, you can always count on your squad. And your squad should always be able to count on you." She shot me a look.

"I know."

"Good. When do you feel you might be ready to come back to us?" She winked. "It might do you good to get back to your regular routine. Doctors say that's the best thing for an upset." She bounced on her feet as if she had so much energy that she couldn't stop herself.

Nora's death had been downgraded to an upset, and I was now supposed to take advice that I was pretty sure she'd gotten from the latest issue of *Good Housekeeping* magazine. "I didn't really have a time line in mind." She had me backed up against the water fountain. The hall was starting to feel a lot more like an interrogation chamber.

Coach looked down her nose at me. "Are you sure this isn't about Shannon and Colton? You know how I feel about letting boys get between friends. Boys come and go, but the friendships you make can last a lifetime."

Her words stopped my heart. I could see her mouth moving, but I was still stuck on what she had just said. Shannon and Colton? Whoa. I swallowed and hoped I was able to keep my face blank. It was clear she thought I knew what she was talking about, and there was no way I was going to admit anything different. My heart skipped a few beats before it picked up its regular rhythm. I forced my chin up in the air. "This has nothing to do with them."

She smiled. "Good. There's a basketball game this weekend. We'll look forward to having you back."

"I'm not sure—" I started to say.

"You know the handbook lists that no squad member is allowed to miss more than four practices or games in a year. I've let this go on because of the unique situation, but your team needs you." She tapped her finger on the copy of the handbook in her arms. Maybe she thought I wasn't going to believe her and she'd have to show it to me in black and white.

I stared at her with my mouth open. "You'd kick me off the squad?" The injustice of it all burned white hot in the center of my chest. I'd never missed a practice before this year. I even showed up at regionals last year when I had the flu. I did that stupid dance routine with a fever of a hundred and one. I was always the one who volunteered to stay after school and paint posters for the hallways without having to be asked. Now I'd missed a few weeks of practice and a single football game, and I wasn't pulling my weight?

Coach Kerr arched one eyebrow. "This is the cheer squad, not dramatics. Let's not get all worked up. I don't plan to kick you off. You're a part of this team, but there's no—" She paused and waited for me to fill it in.

"There's no *I* in team." My voice came out flat.

She clapped her hands together as if I'd answered a particularly tricky question. "Exactly! The choice to be on the team is in your hands."

"I don't—"

She cut me off. "Take time to think about it, because I'm

going to hold you to your decision. This is your choice. It's up to you what you want to do. I like having you on the squad, but that's the issue. I want you on it. Not hanging on to the sidelines. I hope I'll see you at practice tomorrow." She turned and started walking back to her office. Conversation over.

I took a sip of water from the fountain to give myself a second to think. As soon as I stood back up I practically ran right into Shannon and Colton. They were laughing about something, a shared joke. They were near enough that their hips were almost touching. Shannon froze when she saw me, but Colton looked almost glad. Shannon took a step to the side so they weren't so close, but it was too late. It was obvious they'd hooked up. They practically had a neon sign flashing above them, announcing THESE TWO PEOPLE HAVE MADE OUT. How had I missed it? My throat tightened until it felt like someone had me in a choke hold. I could feel the crowd in the hall moving around us in a constant stream, but I was standing still. Everything in my life was moving on.

I bolted for the bathroom. I rushed past a group of sophomore girls huddled around the mirror and slammed the stall door closed. I thought I might vomit. I stood over the toilet, swallowing over and over until the feeling went away. The smell of bleach and the lemon cleaner that the janitors used filled my head. I heard the bathroom door open, and the girls slipped out.

"Avery?" I could see Shannon's sneakers under the stall

door. She'd done up her sneakers with orange and black laces. She must have come in when they left.

I didn't say anything. I didn't know what to say, and I was also afraid if I opened my mouth, I might start screaming. Or throw up. Or both. And then I wouldn't be able to stop. They'd send Bradshaw in to deal with me, and I'd be stuck listening to a lecture on how Wonder Woman worked solo and was just fine on her own.

"We should talk," Shannon said, her fingernail tapping on the metal door. She waited for me to say something. "You guys split up. You even said you didn't want to get back together with him the other day. You said you didn't love him. He's been really down, especially with—you know—what happened after." She sighed. "We sat together at the movie and it just sort of clicked. We were talking about you guys, and how he was feeling like he'd hadn't been there for you and that made him a bad guy. We'd had a bunch of beer and I wasn't thinking clearly. I never planned it. I was going to talk to you and tell you myself. I swear to God."

It felt like my knees weren't going to hold me, like I might fold up like the old map my dad kept in the car. I leaned against the stall for support. When my eyes closed, I could picture the two of them in the dark theater, their arms wrapped around each other. Everyone in our group whispering. No one had told me about it. I suppose it wasn't the kind of news anyone wanted to share. Were they planning to break the news to me in the spring when they went to prom together?

"Say something," Shannon pleaded. "You can yell at me if you want. I'd feel better if you yelled."

I couldn't really be mad at her. She was right; Colton and I had broken up. I didn't want to go to the movie with them. I didn't want to get back together with Colton. It wasn't as if I was staying up late crying into my pillow. It wasn't exactly fair for me to expect that Colton would sit around by himself, but I hadn't expected him to get together with one of my best friends, either. I closed my eyes. I'd always known Shannon liked Colton. The way she talked about him or times I'd catch her looking at him. She should have been the one to go out with him in the first place. I concentrated on breathing slowly in through my nose and out through my mouth. I wanted to explain I wasn't mad at her. I was upset because things in my life kept shifting and changing and I didn't know what I could hold on to anymore. I didn't want to get back with Colton, but part of me had liked knowing that I could. Now that door was shut.

"You have to know I'd never have kissed him if you guys had still been going out. Never."

I nodded, even though I knew she couldn't see me.

"I don't want you to be mad at me. We've been friends for too long. If you don't want me to see him again, I won't. I swear to God. Say the word and that will be it."

It would be too. Shannon wasn't the kind to make a promise and not keep it. Her dad had been in the military before she was born, and he was still really big on things like giving your word. He had a statue of John Wayne in his office and quoted war movies on topics like valor and courage. In junior high Shannon once started crying because she'd promised to sell three cases of Girl Scout cookies and hadn't been able to do it, and she was afraid of what her dad would do when he found out.

"I feel like shit," Shannon said. I could hear that she'd started crying. "Say something so I know you're okay."

I opened my mouth to tell her I was all right. Or at the very least that what was wrong with me wasn't her fault, but nothing came out.

I squeezed my eyes shut to keep from crying. The bell for class rang. I unlocked the stall door, but by the time I opened it, the bathroom door was already swinging shut. Shannon was gone.

chapter nineteen

Brody invited me over so we could try some new options to search for my birth mom. No one had e-mailed me from the adoption groups, and I think we both suspected if it hadn't happened right away, it wasn't going to. We needed to try a different plan. I wasn't sure my parents checked my computer history, but it seemed possible. I didn't want to take the chance of them knowing exactly what was happening with my search. If I cleared my history, it would all but scream, *HEY! I'm doing something that I don't want you to know about.* My parents hadn't asked me a thing about my senior project. It was weird, because normally they couldn't help obsessing about what I did in school. My mom actually made a list of all the books I had to read in English class so she could read them too in case I wanted to talk about them. All of us avoided the topic. The Scott family wasn't great with conflict and unpleasant things. It was like when my cousin Sarah went to rehab, everyone in the family called it "her little break" as if she'd gone off to a spa instead.

I watched Brody as he focused on the screen. He had just gotten out of the shower when I arrived. He smelled like soap, and the hair at the back of his neck was still damp. I fought the urge to snuggle my head into the warm space between his neck and shoulder.

I suspected his room had been a guest room in his aunt and uncle's house before he and his mom moved in last year. The whole house had clearly been a kid-free zone at one time. Too clean and streamlined, almost hotel-like. Not that his aunt and uncle seemed like bad people. His aunt had greeted me at the door. She was freakishly petite, like an elf. I wondered if she had to buy her clothes in the kids' section. I had the sense Brody didn't have many people over and that she was excited to see me. She practically offered to have a parade in my honor as we marched back to his room, and I told her that we had a project we needed to work on for school. I could tell teens made her nervous, like we were some type of exotic creature— interesting, but with the potential to bite.

There were no posters stuck to his walls. Instead there was flocked navy paisley wallpaper. The pictures on the walls were vintage travel posters. They were cool, but they didn't seem like something he would have picked. The only sign that he lived there were the stacks of things on the desk and dresser: photography magazines, a couple of fantasy paperbacks, a digital camera, and a few candy-bar wrappers. I wondered how it would feel to live here, if he felt like a guest all the time. Out of place. I wanted to ask him why he never bothered to make the space his own, but I didn't know how to phrase the question.

There was a giant aquarium against one wall that held a school of brightly colored tropical fish. An air pump made bubbles in the water, and the fish seemed to like diving in and out of them. "This is nice," I said, tapping on the glass.

"It belongs to my uncle. He used this room as his office. He said the gurgling was relaxing. He thought I'd like it." Brody didn't look up from the computer. "My mom talks about how we'll move out and get our own place. This was supposed to be temporary, but she sometimes works nights, so she feels better knowing my aunt and uncle are around. I think she's afraid if I was on my own, I'd have wild parties."

I tried to picture Brody standing on a coffee table, dancing drunk, while people did shots behind him. "She doesn't know you very well, does she?" I asked.

"Not at all." He shifted in his seat. "Things better with you and Shannon?"

I sensed he wanted to change the subject more than he wanted to know about my friend drama. "Things are okay. Lydia had a friend intervention."

He nodded and went back to what he was doing. A large

yellow-and-black fish with lacy fins came up to the glass and seemed to follow my finger. I had the sense the fish was watching me. Like I was the one trapped inside a tank.

"Now, that's interesting," he said. Brody leaned back and cracked his knuckles.

"What did you find?" I turned away from the tank.

"Okay, using the info you brought, we know your birth mom was sixteen the year you were born, which would have made her a junior. We know her name was Lisa." Brody ticked off the facts on his fingers. "In the facts and info sheet she filled out for the adoption agency, she talked about how she loved competitive swimming."

"So all we need to do is track down every sixteen-year-old in America at that time who liked the water." I leaned back against his bed. "Are you planning to track swimsuit sales?"

"No, and we don't have to search all of America. We can almost bet she lived in Michigan too. Your parents picked you up at their lawyer's office here in Lansing when you were just a couple days old. Now, it's possible they move babies all around the country, but I'm guessing most of the time they're in-state adoptions."

"Fair enough," I agreed.

"So you were born in May, which means if your mom wanted, she could have returned for the competitive swim season in her senior year."

"I guess."

"Now, I don't know much about your birth mom, but I know a bit about you. You don't tend to do things halfway, and I bet she didn't either. So I'm guessing she didn't just like to swim. She liked to swim and win. So I pulled up the state swim-meet results for the year after you were born, assuming she would have gone back to it." He turned his laptop to face me.

I kneeled next to his computer chair. There, listed as having come in second in the breaststroke, was a Lisa Moriarty from Southside High School.

Brody scrolled down. "She came in first in the fifty meter."

My finger lightly touched the screen. Moriarty. It was an Irish name. Maybe that's why I liked St. Patrick's Day so much.

"Now, hang on—there's three more." He clicked over to another page. Lisa Bucain was listed. "This Lisa was on the relay team that took first. She's from a high school outside Detroit." He clicked again. "There's a Lisa Watkowski from Dearborn who was in the one hundred meter, and a Lisa Blackmoore from Traverse City."

"Four. That's not that bad," I said, trying to keep the excitement out of my voice.

Brody leaned back in his chair. "There are three other Lisas who were in diving competitions."

"But she doesn't say diving on the interest form," I argued. "She clearly says competitive swimming."

"True, I'm just pointing out that it's an option. She did mention in the letter to you that she did a high dive. She might not have competed, but there's a chance she did. The other thing is that there are probably lots of girls named Lisa who swam and didn't win anything. I'm just making the assumption that she would be a winner."

My initial rush of excitement was starting to fade.

Brody nudged my shoulder. "Don't give up so easy. It might not be the answer, but it's a place to start. It gives us something to chase down. It's more than we had an hour ago."

"So, do we call the schools they went to and see if they remember if the Lisa that went there eighteen years ago was pregnant the year before she won? It doesn't seem likely they'd remember. There might not be anyone working at the school who was even there back then."

"I was thinking we go to the schools and check out the old yearbooks. I figure we may get really lucky, and one of the Lisas will obviously not be your mom because she'll be Chinese or something, or you might look just like one of them," Brody said.

My heart pumped overtime. Growing up I used to hate when people met my parents for the first time. They would look at my mom and then my dad, trying to figure out where my looks came from. Then they would hear I was adopted and you could almost see the *ah, that explains it* on their face. The idea that there could be someone out there who looked like me was intoxicating. Another idea popped into my head. "If we check the yearbook for the year before, we might be able to tell which is the right Lisa. If she wasn't on the swim team in her junior year, for example. Or she might have dropped out altogether and been homeschooled."

"Exactly. So what do you say? We've got Christmas break coming up. Road trip?"

"Nothing says adventure like a trip around Michigan in the winter. I'll pay for snacks, and we can take my car," I offered.

"I never turn down an offer of pork rinds."

"You like those things? They're disgusting." My nose wrinkled.

Brody placed his hand over his heart as if mortally wounded. "You would trash-talk a man's pork rinds? His go-to salty snack?" He shook his head sadly.

"Will the schools be open?"

"Our break starts a bit early because of the professional development day the teachers are taking. I'm betting most schools don't start their vacation until the following Monday. If we're lucky, we've got a couple of days when we're out and they'll still be in school."

"A couple of days isn't a lot of time." I started to try and sort the route in my head.

"Would your parents let you stay the night someplace?"

A sliver of excitement ran down my spine. Did he want to stay somewhere with me? An image of lying next to him in bed flashed in my head. Then in the next instant I pictured telling my folks I wanted to take a road trip with a guy. I flopped over on the floor. *Shit.* "No. My parents will freak out. They don't like me driving around town in the winter, let alone on the highway. And staying over? No way."

"Don't get so bummed. We'll think of something." Brody nudged my leg with his foot. "You didn't strike me as the type to give up easy."

"I guess I don't know what type I am; that's the problem," I admitted.

Brody got down on the floor and sat next to me. I was hyper aware of the feeling of his leg against mine. "Is this because we're looking for your birth mom?"

"No. Yes. Maybe a little."

Brody chuckled. "Well, that narrows it down."

"The thing is, growing up, Nora was the one who was really obsessed with finding her birth mom. I was curious, but I didn't feel like I had a good reason to be interested. She had no history, not even a hint. Why my mom gave me up wasn't too hard to figure out. She was still in high school. Nora had nothing."

"It could be that you felt your mom made the best decision she could, that she wanted you to have a good life and that you didn't need to find her."

I listened to the gurgle of the fish tank. "I think that's what I wanted to believe, but what if I didn't want to find my birth mom because I was afraid of what I might find out?"

Brody seemed to think about it. "I'm pretty sure if she was a serial killer, that's the kind of thing that would have been listed."

I poked him with my elbow. "Thanks for reassuring me that I'm not likely to start keeping dead people in my freezer."

"Hey now, I didn't say that. You might like to dress up like a clown and peel kittens, for all I know. I'm just pointing out it's not likely genetic."

"I sometimes think I didn't want to look for my birth mom because I didn't want to highlight the fact I'm adopted. Like I'm trying to convince everyone that I am who I'm always pretending to be. Fake it until I make it kind of thing."

"What's wrong with who you are? Why do you have to fake anything?"

I felt myself flush. "Are you saying that you don't ever wish to be someone else?" I asked him.

"You mean other than Batman?"

I rolled my eyes. "Yes, Caped Crusader, other than being Batman, don't you sometimes feel like you're falling short of what people expect of you?"

"It's sort of hard to fall short of nothing. My dad doesn't even remember I'm alive, and my mom's expectation is that I don't get into trouble. Short of following in your footsteps and becoming a killer clown, she's happy."

I sighed. I wasn't sure what was worse, feeling like I was failing compared to what everyone expected, or feeling like your family expected you to fail. "Maybe we're both screwed up," I suggested.

"Only in the best way."

I stared at him in mock shock. "Kind words? Are you being a gentleman?"

"What's wrong with being a gentleman?"

"Nothing's wrong. I'm just not used to it." I picked at the carpet nap and bit the inside of my lip. I wanted him to make a move on me, but I couldn't shake the idea that he wouldn't. He'd wait for me. "Course, if you weren't such a gentleman, you could be kissing me now." I held my breath. *Oh God, what if I totally misread the situation?*

His eyes were wide. I'd managed to shock him if nothing else. He leaned forward. "I'm a gentleman, but it's still sort of a work in progress." He kissed me. Then he sat back as if waiting to see if it was okay. His hand was shaking. I pulled his face closer to me and kissed him. He wound his hands into my hair, bringing my face to his to kiss me again. His mouth opened under mine. It wasn't a kiss; it was a consuming.

chapter twenty

Time is a weird thing. If you're stuck in a dentist chair for a root canal, a half hour can seem like an entire day. Summer vacation can seem to last forever, until it's the last day and then you realize it flew by. Kissing Brody was like that; time went off the tracks. Lost its meaning. It was as if I had always been there, next to him, and it also passed in a blink. Unlike with Colton, with Brody I felt liquid. Electric and liquid all at the same time. I would have still been kissing him except his aunt knocked on the door, which broke the spell.

"Does Avery want to stay for dinner?" she asked.

The skin around my mouth felt slightly raw from where his whiskers had rubbed. I touched my lips lightly with my finger. Then I saw the clock on his bedside table.

"Shit, is that the time?" I scrambled to get up from the

floor. "The basketball game starts in thirty minutes." I threw my things in my bag.

Brody watched me, confused. "I had no idea you were this big a basketball fan."

"No. I'm cheering. Long story, but I promised I'd be there."

Brody grabbed the strap of my bag and pulled me back for one more kiss. "Are you going to be in trouble for being late?"

"Maybe." I smiled. "It might be worth it."

"Might?" His lip curled into a smile, and I kissed him again quickly before throwing open his bedroom door. I apologized to his aunt as I ran out the door. I knew Coach Kerr would be ticked I was late. I'd been at the past few practices, but this was my first game back. One of the squad rules was consideration. If you were going to be late, you were supposed to call. Telling her I'd been making out and had lost all sense of time wasn't going to go over well.

I burst out of the girls' locker room and bolted across the gym floor to join the rest of the squad. The bleachers were already full. Coach Kerr glanced at me and then made a point to look at the clock on the wall, and back again at me.

Lydia squealed and hugged me like I'd returned from war. Shannon and I stood awkwardly next to each other for a beat before she hugged me too. Lydia had made us talk everything out. There was nothing she hated more than conflict. The idea of her two best friends not getting along was enough to bring on a full-fledged panic attack for the poor girl. We'd sorted things out, but it was still awkward. We were acting like nothing had changed, but it had. Sometimes I wished a car would hit me so I'd have amnesia and have no memory of how it used to be. It says a lot about my life that a brain injury seemed preferable to what I had now.

Coach Kerr looked at the clock again. "Last time I checked, the agreement was that the squad was here a half hour before any game," she said.

I knew what was required—groveling. "I had trouble with my car," I lied. "Not that it's any excuse. It's totally my fault. I completely understand if you want to leave Liz in tonight. I'm just glad to be here with you guys." I stared down at my shoes and tried to look sufficiently pathetic. I was having a hard time not smiling and bouncing in place. Brody had kissed me. He liked me. I tried to focus on Coach.

"I trust this will be the last time you'll be late." Coach tapped her foot on the parquet floor. "The team counts on us. We provide them with hope. It's our job to step into the breach, no matter if we're tired, or feeling under the weather, or have car trouble."

Shannon and Lydia were both doing their best not to giggle. I think we all expected Coach to suddenly start beating her chest and have movie music swell up in the background as she gave her "cheerleading saves lives" talk.

"Okay, you're in," Coach said. "I want to see you give one hundred percent tonight."

"At least one hundred twenty percent," I fired back, trying to match her perky tone. I must have done something right, because she smiled. Lydia reached over and squeezed my hand.

"Ready?" Shannon yelled out.

"Set," the rest of us screamed back.

"Go!" We ran out into the center of the gym floor and hit our marks. Coach turned on our music and it blared from the giant speakers. I'd only been back for two practices. The morning after the first one I felt so stiff I wasn't sure I would be able to get out of bed. It felt like someone had poured quick-dry cement in my veins overnight. Our squad had a set of routines we did during football, but during basketball they were more complicated. Cheering for football was about volume and being careful not to do anything where you might fall on the wet grass. Basketball meant we'd be inside in a climate-controlled space where we could do more of the routines we did for competitions. Some of it had come back easily; I'd been cheering since ninth grade, so most of the moves were muscle memory by now. Other times I felt like I was hopelessly out of sync with the rest of the group—like I was in an early round of *So You Think You Can Dance* where the answer was clearly no.

Shannon was our captain, so she led us through the first chant, our claps tight and in rhythm. We got the crowd yelling back and moved quickly into a basket toss. I was a base. Flyers might get all the glory, but I wasn't keen on people tossing me into the air above a hardwood floor. Stacey was our flyer and she was perfect for it. She could fold herself into a tight nugget, had perfect balance, and could smile even through total terror.

I smiled out at the crowd and saw my parents. They were sitting together near the players' bench. Mom waved madly at me. I nodded to let her know I saw them. If I waved, Coach would come over and amputate my arm at the shoulder for breaking the routine. I could tell they were both glad to see me back on the squad.

Stacey did a dead man fall, and I stepped forward to catch her with Shannon. I had an instant where I pictured her falling, breaking through our hold and smacking into the floor, her bones snapping. I must have blinked, because in the next second she was already in our arms.

The music changed, and the announcer came over the loudspeaker. The team was going to come out. We moved into two lines, forming a spirited tunnel for the players to run through. They called out the lead players, and we shook our pompons for all they were worth. When Colton's name was called, I felt myself stiffen. Last year at this time we'd just started going out. We'd done this thing where he would high-five my pompon as he ran through. I focused on staring straight ahead and smiling like my life depended on it. He ran past me without glancing. He didn't high-five Shannon, but he did wink. I took a deep breath. I could do this.

Near the end of the fourth quarter I was already wiped out. My ears were ringing from all the noise, and my hands stung from clapping. The scoreboard showed we still had two minutes to go with no more time-outs. Our team was ahead, but only by six points. We were playing Taft High. Apparently the Vikings didn't know that they should give up so I could have a rest. We were kneeling on the sidelines, waiting for a break in play or game end so we could go start another chant. I switched knees on the floor, trying to ignore the shooting pain that was going up my leg. I tried to forget that I could have stayed at Brody's place, kissing him, instead of being here.

Coach clapped me on the shoulder and whispered in my ear, "Feels good to be back, doesn't it?"

I nodded. Not really. What it felt like was that my leg was going to fall off.

Stacey leaned over after she walked away. "I'm glad you're here. It wasn't the same without you."

"Thanks." I wished I felt as excited to be back as everyone else seemed to be to have me around. I remembered when I'd gotten onto the team as a freshman, I'd been thrilled. It was like I'd won the lotto. I knew my gymnastics experience would give me an edge; that much was obvious at tryouts, but it was still no guarantee.

Nora had had no idea why I cared.

"Seriously? You want to prance around in a short skirt and cheer boys on to do things?" Nora's face scrunched up. "What's up next, repealing the right to vote? Having your feet bound?"

"There's nothing wrong with cheer. It'll look great on my college apps." I crossed my arms.

"Sure. Knock yourself out. I didn't see you as someone who would like cheerleading, that's all."

"Well, I do," I insisted.

Looking back, I wasn't sure if I was trying to convince her or myself.

Getting on the squad was the final straw for the friendship I had with Nora. There was no big fight, no screaming match where we declared that the other person was dead to us. It was more that cheer took up so much time, and that I *liked* being a part of the squad. I didn't want to hang out with Nora, because it highlighted how I didn't fit with the rest of the cheerleaders. It was easier to be with Shannon and Lydia. I enjoyed how people turned to look at us when we walked down the hall in our uniforms. Maybe I figured if they were looking at the uniform, they wouldn't look too closely at me. Now I was starting to like the idea of being seen.

The buzzer rang, shocking me out of my thoughts. I was so startled I fell over off my knee and onto my ass. I scrambled to get up and join the rest of the squad in the middle of the floor. My leg had fallen asleep, and I had to drag it behind me as I ran out. The rest of the squad bounced around, shaking one of their pompons in the air.

"Smooth, Scott," Shannon said, smiling.

"I was sort of hoping no one noticed."

Shannon laughed. "Haven't you figured it out? Everyone's always watching."

Colton ran off the players' bench and picked up Shannon. She whacked him on the back so he'd put her down. Coach wasn't keen on public displays of affection. I turned away and pretended an interest in the crowd. The players jogged off the floor. The Vikings had already gone into the locker room. They hadn't stayed to shake hands. It could be they were sore losers, or they wanted to hit the showers so they could get on the road. They were predicting snow. I was ready to go home, but Coach Kerr didn't like us to leave until the last of the crowd left. Peppy to the end. That was us.

"Good job, girls!" Coach came over. "A few of you need to work on your liberty moves; I saw some shaky legs out there. Let's keep things crisp and clean."

We all nodded in unison.

"I did notice something else," Coach said. She pointed down at Stacey's shoes. "Those are looking a bit scuffed."

Stacey shifted uncomfortably. The rule was that we weren't supposed to wear our court shoes outside, under pain of death. Anything less than blindingly white sneakers was a sign quality was slipping. Today scuffed sneakers, tomorrow we'd start mainlining heroin.

"I accidentally wore them out the other day," Stacey admitted. "I polished them up when I got home."

Coach Kerr didn't answer her. She didn't have to. The message had been sent. Stacey had been up on top of the pyramid

with shoddy shoes. She might as well have been up there com-
mando, flashing the crowd.

"Avery, nice job out there for your first time back, but you
looked a bit off your game. Stay sharp."

Considering I'd fallen over at the end buzzer, I was getting
off easy. Must be the last of my sympathy points.

"I have some news for you girls. As you know, Ms. Harmen,
the biology teacher, has been diagnosed with breast cancer. The
school is doing some various fund-raisers for her and her family
and also to raise awareness. Naturally, when the topic came up
at the faculty meeting, I thought of our group. A lot of people
look up to us, so we can do our part to help out."

I mentally crossed my fingers and hoped this didn't mean
we would have to do a car wash in the middle of December or
be forced to sell cheap candy bars door-to-door to raise money.

Coach Kerr reached behind her back and pulled out a large
plastic shopping bag. She began to pass out hot-pink knee-
highs to each of us. "Next week we're going to wear these with
our uniforms. Along with these pins." She passed each of us a
small pink ribbon pin.

The pin sat in the palm of my hand. I wondered if Ms.
Harmen, or anyone with breast cancer for that matter, really
felt cheered up by being surrounded by pink. Ms. Harmen
lived with her partner, Jill, and seemed like someone who was
born to teach high school biology. She actually got giddy when
it was time for the dissection lab. No one should be that excited
by frog intestines. She drove a giant red pickup truck that took

up nearly two parking stalls in the faculty lot. I couldn't imagine that her finding us wandering the halls in pink socks was going to do much to improve her mood or make her feel any better. Cancer sucked. Dressing it up didn't make it better, in my opinion, but what did I know? I'd never known anyone personally who had the disease.

The realization came to me in a rush. I dropped my pin. That was it. I knew how to find my birth mom.

chapter twenty-one

For the first time in my life I'd been glad my parents gave me the curfew of an elementary school kid. I'd tried telling them that the only seniors who had to be home by midnight on a weekend were either homeschooled religious types or those who needed special education, but they hadn't gone for it. Last night I'd been happy to sigh dramatically and declare that I'd have to call it a night. I'd wanted to go home right after the game, but there was no way to skip out on the postgame pizza bash. The players were hyped up from the win, and a few of them were already talking about how this could be the year they went all the way to state finals. Given that we'd only played a handful of games so far, it seemed a bit of a stretch. I focused on smiling and acting like there was no place I'd rather be. Shannon sat on Colton's lap, and I could feel everyone turn slightly to see how I would react. That also meant I couldn't leave early, because I didn't want people thinking I was leaving because it bothered me. I checked my phone compulsively so I could see the time, and as soon as it seemed reasonable, I made my excuses and ducked out.

As soon as I got home, I shucked off my cheerleading uniform and fired up my laptop. It seemed like I should say a prayer or have some kind of ceremony to ensure that my idea worked out, but I didn't think religion had a plan to cover this type of situation. I pulled out my bag and the list I'd made at Brody's. I read through each name again and then started the search.

The secret to searching for something on the Internet, or in life in general, is to know what you're looking for. That would have helped. All I had was a vague idea and hope. Around three a.m. I was ready to give up. In the morning I'd call Brody and see if he had any other ideas of where to look. I was just about ready to click off the computer when I saw her name. I rubbed my eyes to make sure it wasn't an exhaustion-induced hallucination, but when I opened them again, her name was still there. I jumped up and danced around my bed. I wanted to let out a whoop, but I was pretty sure my parents wouldn't be interested in sharing my celebration and certainly not at this hour. I pulled my phone out to text Brody. There was already a text from him.

Lunch tomorrow at El Az?

I texted back yes and then threw myself across the bed. This had to be it. I rolled back and forth on the bed, hugging myself. I eventually turned out the light, but I couldn't sleep. It was like I'd drunk an entire case of Red Bull and tossed it back with a pot of coffee. My body was practically vibrating with energy. I'd found my mom. I was sure of it. I closed my eyes and pictured making the presentation with Brody, with the admissions people from Duke in the audience. Everyone would be moved to tears. The idea that I'd found my mom and kept my promise to Nora. There were made-for-TV movies that didn't have this much drama. The admissions people would basically drop to their knees and plead for me to go to Duke.

I flipped my pillow over to get to the cool side. My parents wouldn't be thrilled that I'd found her, but when they realized how what I'd done was going to get me into Duke, they'd understand. I wasn't planning to move in with Lisa. Just sit down with her. Talk a bit. Maybe exchange Christmas cards every year or something.

I rolled onto my other side. What would Nora think if she were still around? Would she be happy for me, or would she feel like it wasn't fair? She was the one who had been so sure if she could find her birth mom that somehow the universe would fall into place and her life would suddenly make sense.

I found my birth mom. I held my pillow to my face and smothered a small yell. It wasn't just about Duke anymore.

. . .

It was a good thing I'd set an alarm, or I would have slept through lunch. The last time I could remember looking at the clock was five thirty, when I heard my mom get up for her run. I felt like my head was stuffed with wet cotton and my hands weren't fully connected to my arms. No wonder sleep deprivation can be used as torture.

I walked into El Azteco and Brody raised a hand. My heart gave an extra thump when I saw him. He'd already snagged a table. I slid into the booth. Brody passed me one of the laminated menus. I didn't have to look; I already knew I wanted the spicy *enchiladas de jocoque*, my favorite. El Az had been around in East Lansing forever. If you wanted great Mexican, there wasn't a better place in town.

Brody dipped his chip into the hot salsa and then pushed the bowl over to me. "Do you want to try and catch a movie after? Since this sort of counts as our first official date, it seems we should do more than lunch."

My stomach jumped. This was an official date, wasn't it? This day kept getting better. "Doesn't matter what we do after." I leaned forward, excited. "Guess what I figured out last night?"

"That you find my charm irresistible?" He struck a pose.

I cocked an eyebrow. "I think we established yesterday when I kissed you that I found you charming. No, this is big news. Last night I had this flash of inspiration. I'm pretty sure I found my birth mom."

Brody went from joking to serious. "Are you sure? Did someone contact you?"

"Nope. This was pure brilliance." I yanked a paper out of my bag. "This form was in my adoption scrapbook. My birth mom was supposed to list any family health issues."

"Having a medical history is one of the perks of an open adoption." Brody looked over the sheet. "Looks pretty straightforward. I take it you're happy there's no history of mental illness?"

"It's a bonus, but it's not what caught my eye. See this?" I pointed at the page.

"Your grandmother had breast cancer."

"You've heard that Ms. Harmen has breast cancer too, right?"

Brody paused his chip above the salsa bowl. "You think you're related to the biology teacher? You know lots of people in Michigan get cancer, right?"

I tossed the napkin in my lap at him. "No, I don't think I'm related to our biology teacher. Hearing about her is just what got me thinking about it. My grandma didn't die of it," I pointed out. "She's listed as still alive when I was born, in her forties."

Brody looked at me. "I guess that's a good thing. Always nice to have an extra grandparent. She was only in her forties when she became a grandma, bet that freaked her out. Where are you going with this?"

"It would be important to my birth mom, wouldn't it? If her mom, my grandma, fought breast cancer when she was a kid, that would have made a big impression on her."

Brody nodded. "Sure. Makes sense."

"So that got me thinking: What would I do if my mom had breast cancer?" I couldn't keep the smile off my face. I couldn't tell if I was happier with what I had figured out or the fact that my birth mom and I clearly thought the same way. "The Michigan Cancer Society keeps great records. The year after I was born they did one of those Race for the Cure–type things."

"And?"

"Check out the youth-teams coordinator." I pulled out another sheet I'd printed off the computer. I pointed at the name Lisa Moriarty. "She did it for her mom," I whispered. I repeated her name in my head. *Lisa Moriarty.* "It has to be her, don't you think? Otherwise it's way too much of a coincidence. She was a competitive swimmer. And then this."

Brody smiled at me across the table. "Nice going, Sherlock. You can't say for sure it's her, but it sounds likely to me. It's a good start."

"Start?" I felt my enthusiasm sink a notch.

"Assuming Lisa Moriarty is your birth mom, it doesn't mean that's her name anymore. She might be married and go by her husband's name, or she might have moved to Arizona or Paris, France, for all we know. We haven't found her yet."

I felt a flush of annoyance. "I know, but I'm close. I can

tell. At least we don't have to figure out how to squeeze in a tour of the entire state of Michigan. We can start with Southside, and if I'm right, we're done. I still want to check out the yearbook, and I have an idea about getting her married name too."

Brody reached over and touched my hand lightly. "I didn't mean to tick you off. I know this is a big deal. I only want to make sure that you don't get ahead of yourself. We're still a long way from finding her. Things could go sideways." He held up a hand. "Don't get me wrong; I'm not saying they will. What you found out is huge. But I don't want you to get hurt."

I could see the concern in his eyes, and the annoyance I'd felt melted away. "I don't plan to get hurt."

"No one plans on it." He sat back as the waitress brought our food. The plates nearly bounced on the table as she dropped them. My nose twitched at the smell of peppers—I was suddenly starving. Brody motioned for me to grab a fork. "We can't do anything else today because of the weekend. We can go to Southside next Thursday and make our plan from there."

"I was thinking we could go on Monday. It won't be a huge deal if we skip; most of the teachers are coasting next week. Who wants to get into anything before the holidays, anyway? That way we can finish up our project over the Christmas break."

"Avery Scott skipping class? Isn't that a sign of the end of times?" Brody teased me. "It's only a few days. We can wait until Thursday. We have until the end of February to finish the project."

My foot bounced under the table. I couldn't tell him that the Duke interview deadline was looming. I needed to get this done. I ate my enchiladas, burning my mouth on the molten cheese while I tried to figure out if I could come up with an excuse why we had to do it now.

"Since you're on a roll with solving mysteries, what about if we rent a movie? You ever see *The Maltese Falcon*?" I shook my head. "It's good. I have a bit of a TMC addiction. I get insomnia a lot, so it's either old movies or infomercials. Netflix will have it."

"I hate when I can't sleep." I slid the red plastic tumbler over to the edge of the table so the waitress would know I wanted more water. El Az might be an institution in town, but it wasn't exactly five-star service. We were lucky our tabletop wasn't sticky. "Last night I kept looking at the clock and calculating how much sleep I'd get if I fell asleep at exactly that moment. I'll get five hours forty-three minutes of sleep, now only five hours and forty-two minutes, forty-one minutes. The whole thing makes me anxious, which makes it even harder to drift off."

"The secret is, if you can't sleep, get up. It's less frustrating. It's weird because you know you're awake when so few are. It's like a post-apocalyptic world filled with very few, and very odd, people. You get to belong to a secret club, the night people. Once last summer I got up and drove to Walmart because I wanted to get out of the house, and it was the only place I could think of that was open. There were, like, four people in the store, and two of them were working. The other customer was this guy in his fifties who was wearing hot-pink leggings and a cowboy hat." He raised his hand as if taking a vow. "I'm not even making that up. I have a picture somewhere."

"Maybe I should start hanging out at the Walmart in the middle of the night."

"I have this theory that artistic people are more likely to have insomnia. Something with the creative brain turning on when our day-to-day brain finally turns off." Brody scooped some refried beans onto his taco.

"Have you thought more about art college?" I asked him.

"I don't know. I'm hoping my time bumming around Europe and New York will help me sort it out. New York's the city that never sleeps, after all." He smiled. There was a small smear of salsa above his lip. "You know how I like the nonsleepers. Besides, you know I'm not a huge college fan. You're not going to see me chasing after someone for their approval."

I knew he wanted to change the subject, so I dropped it. "Well, then you're going to love me—I haven't slept in days. I should warn you I might nod off in the middle of the movie."

"I won't take it as a comment on how exciting it is to be with me." He winked at me. "Maybe I'll think of something to keep you awake. Keep you from getting bored during the movie."

I blushed as an image of him kissing me came into my head. "Are you using the excuse of a movie to get me in a dark room?"

"Do I get points for honesty? Because, yep, pretty much."

I laughed. "Well then, let's go as soon as we finish lunch."

Brody raised his hand to flag the waitress. "Can we get the rest of this to go?"

chapter twenty-two

For my first piece of fake ID, I thought it looked pretty good. I concentrated on giving the school secretary my best "future leader of tomorrow" smile.

I glanced at the clock on the wall. I still had plenty of time, but every second the clock ticked over sounded loud, like how bomb timers sounded in movies. Sunday night I'd decided I couldn't wait until Thursday the way Brody wanted. I wandered around the house letting out a fake cough every so often and grumbling about feeling tired. This morning I'd given an Oscar-worthy performance of sickness. There was no way I could go to school. I was simply too ill. I'd warmed up my face with a heating pad before going to tell my mom. She'd pressed her cool hand to my forehead and wrinkled up her face in concern. The plan had almost gone south when she declared that maybe she'd work from home that day so she could keep an eye on me. She was worried about my fever. Note to self: Next time stick to a fake cold or a stomachache. A little after ten her office called with some problem, and I announced that I was feeling well enough that she could go.

I waited for twenty minutes after she left in case she'd forgotten something and returned home. When I was sure she wasn't coming back, I pounded up the stairs and jumped into the shower. As soon as I got out I pulled up the directions on my phone and sent my mom an e-mail saying that I was going to take a nap and I was going to turn off the phone. I thought about telling her that I knew sleep was what I needed to feel better, but I thought it might be laying it on too thick.

Even with directions I'd taken a wrong turn trying to find the school. I needed to get the information and get back on the road to make sure I left enough time to beat my parents home.

"Who did you say you were again?" the school secretary asked me.

"Amy Richardson," I lied. I slid my identification farther across the counter so she could see it clearly. Considering I'd made the ID on the computer last night, it looked good to me. I used the Michigan Cancer Society logo off their website and made a badge, adding my title, Director of Youth Programs, underneath. To make it look even better, this morning on the way here I took it to the copy shop and had them laminate it. Everything laminated looks more official. I pointed toward her ancient computer. "If you go on our website, you'll see me listed there."

She would see my name, at least. That was the whole reason I chose the name Amy. It was the real name of the youth-program coordinator. Now, the real Amy might have been forty-five, but thankfully the Cancer Society didn't put pictures up of their staff. All I had to do was hope that I looked old enough to have the job, which was why I'd dressed so carefully this morning in one of my mom's suits and pulled my hair into a French twist that I hoped added a year or two. The school secretary went to her computer and came back after a moment.

"Now, what was it you wanted?"

"The Cancer Society is doing a big banquet to highlight the importance of youth getting involved in community programs. We're hoping to invite some people who made a real difference over the years. One of your past students—" I forced myself to look down at my clipboard as if I couldn't quite recall the name. "Ah, yes, Lisa Moriarty. Lisa did an impressive job when she organized one of the first races to raise money. We would love to have her be a part of the dinner, but unfortunately we've lost track of her over the years. I was hoping, since she's one of your alumni, you'd have her current contact information: phone, address, married name." I waved my hand around as if what I was asking for was no big deal.

"We're not supposed to give out contact information for past students," she hedged, looking uncertain.

"Lisa is the only student from the Southside area that would be a part of the event. It shines such a positive light on your school," I mentioned. "I'm sure school administration stresses volunteer work and community involvement for students. It would be a great promotion for you."

"Community service is one of our core values. It's in our mission statement." I didn't tell her that I knew that from the school website. The secretary looked past me down the hall. "I'd feel better if I could check with our principal, but he just stepped out."

I pressed my mouth into a smile. He had to step out because I had called twenty minutes ago saying I was a student who needed to talk to him confidentially about someone who was selling drugs. I told him I couldn't meet at the school and begged to get together at the coffee shop, Cops & Doughnuts, down the street. That had gotten him out of the office, but he was only going to sit down there by himself for a bit before he figured the whole thing was a ruse. I needed her to cough up the information now.

"Maybe I could call you later today with the details?" the secretary offered.

I tried to look disappointed. "Unfortunately, we have a press release going out this afternoon, so for me to include her and the school on it I'd have to get that information now. That's my fault. I should have stopped by sooner, but things have been crazy with the holidays coming up. I just assumed if

I came with my identification . . ." I let my voice trail off. My finger tapped the laminated badge on the counter. I hoped it looked sufficiently official. Who wouldn't tell the Cancer Society something? If you can't trust people trying to cure cancer, who can you trust?

"Well, I suppose in this kind of case it wouldn't be an issue."

I gave her another smile that I hoped communicated that I wasn't a troublemaker. She sat down at her computer, pulled something up on the screen with just a few clicks, and then wrote something down. I felt my heart speed up. The secretary passed me a small sheet of scrap paper. I did my best not to leap into the air and let out a giant whoop. I tucked it into the stack of paper on my clipboard as if it didn't mean a thing. I was sure that she would be able to look at me and tell I was freaking out, but either I was able to look normal or she wasn't paying attention.

"We don't have a current address. She hasn't kept up with the alumni association, but we do have her married name. You might be able to find her online."

"Thank you so much. I'll be sure to have the Cancer Society send a copy of the press release here." I glanced at my watch as if I had a pile of pressing engagements. "I suppose I should leave and see if I can't find her. Do you mind if I use one of your restrooms before I hit the road?"

"No problem, there's one right down the hall."

I stepped out of the office and moved down the corridor. I

wasn't interested in the bathroom, but I was interested in finding the library. As soon as I cleared the office windows, I pulled out the clipboard. Lisa Deroche. She was married. Or at least she had been at one point. I committed the name to memory so that if anything happened to the paper, I would still know it. I did my best to walk quickly without looking like I was running or tripping over my high heels. I paused long enough to pull my hair out of the updo and peel off the suit jacket so I looked a bit more casual and closer to my own age. I kept the visitor tag the secretary had given me, in case anyone asked for it. I passed by classrooms without bothering to glance inside. The librarian looked up when I walked in. I took a deep breath and got ready to spin another giant whopper of a lie. It was a good thing I used to do all that creative writing with Nora; I needed all the imagination I could get.

"Hi. My family is in town visiting my grandma. My mom used to go to school here. She lost her yearbook years ago when our basement flooded, and I thought it would be neat to copy some pictures out of it for her for Christmas." I rolled my eyes. "My parents are big on homemade gifts. Do you keep old yearbooks?"

"Sure. I wouldn't want to stand in the way of a homemade present." The librarian pointed me over to the reference section. "We keep all the old yearbooks over there. They're on the shelf by year."

I ran my fingers along the spines until I found the right

one. I risked a glance up, but the librarian wasn't watching me. I pulled it out and flipped past the group shots of everyone mugging for the camera until I found the listing for seniors. My heart was beating so loud I was surprised that the librarian couldn't hear it. There were two pages stuck together and I almost ripped them in my excitement, but it was worth it when I pried them apart. There she was, between Brian Moran and Theresa Morin. I swallowed hard. It was a typical senior photo; her hair was a bit overly fluffed, and she had that faraway look that seemed to be required of senior photos, as if you could see your own future just out of frame. My finger traced the lines of her face. We looked alike. There wasn't any doubt. Lisa Moriarty was my mom.

"Do you want me to make a photocopy?" a voice said behind me, making me jump. The librarian stood there smiling. "Students are supposed to have a code from their teacher for the photocopier, but for your mom's trip down memory lane, I'm willing to make a couple copies on the house."

"Yes, please." My voice came out tight and quiet. I almost didn't want to hand over the yearbook, but if I clutched it and ran for the door, that was bound to cause some trouble. I held it out. "This is her. It's my mom. Lisa Moriarty."

She took the book out of my hand and looked at the picture. "Oh, I can tell. You have her eyes."

I thought my heart would explode. "I do, don't I?"

"My kids hate when I tell them how much we look alike."

"I don't mind at all."

"Let me grab a couple copies." She stepped behind her desk and pressed the open yearbook onto a small copier on the counter. Outside the window I could see snow falling. "Here you go."

I took the pages from her hand.

"I looked in the index. Your mom was on the swim team, so I copied their team photo and another shot she was in."

Now that I had seen her photo it was easy to pick her out of the team photo. She was in the back row. She was tall like me. It was her fault I towered over every guy in our class in junior high. The realization made me want to giggle. The other photo the librarian photocopied was a group of kids at what looked like a football game. She was sitting on the shoulders of a cute guy, and her mouth was open, laughing. There was a caption: "Seniors Lisa Moriarty and David Ketchum laugh it up."

"I bet your mom will be thrilled you did this for her," the librarian said. "It's certainly going to be a Christmas surprise."

"I hope so."

chapter twenty-three

I've always been a planner. I like making lists and crossing things off. I may never have skipped school before, but I had planned everything perfectly to ensure the chances of getting caught were almost nonexistent.

Almost.

First, I knew reputation was on my side. I wasn't the kind of kid who skipped. I hardly missed school when I had a legitimate excuse. I was much more the type to stay after class to help the teacher with a project than sneak out. I could have danced out the front door of school yelling *I'm outta here!* at the top of my lungs, and most of the teachers would assume I was just teasing. The second reason I was sure I wouldn't get caught was because my own mom had called the school, letting them know I was going to be out sick. You can't get a better excuse than your own mom.

I knew the time was going to be tight since I'd gotten a later start than I wanted, but Southside was only an hour and a half from East Lansing. The plan would have worked perfectly if the snow hadn't started to dump down. The fresh snow, combined with the wet roads, caused a huge accident on the highway. Everyone was stuck while they cleared the accident, and then, since no one wanted a repeat of what had happened, traffic crawled along even after we passed the spot. I watched the clock in the car ticking forward. I bounced in the seat, trying to mentally wish the traffic out of my way.

I finally got off the highway and raced down my street. It was already starting to get dark, and houses were turning on their holiday lights. I whipped into the driveway. Neither of my parents' cars was out front. I'd made it. I took a deep breath. As I got out of the car, I heard my name. I spun around and saw Brody getting out of his car across the street. He shuffled through the snow.

"You went to Southside, didn't you?"

"I can explain," I said.

"We agreed to do this together. Remember? It was a rule. I would have gone with you on Thursday."

"I know, but I couldn't wait." I wished I could explain to him why, but I knew he wouldn't understand. "What are you doing here?"

"When you didn't show up at school this morning, I tried

calling you and didn't get an answer. I drove around, trying to figure out where you might be. I was going to go to Southside, but I didn't know what story you gave to the school, and I didn't want to ruin it for you."

I winced. He was going to get in trouble for skipping. "I should have told you what I was planning. On the upside, it's a good thing I went today. We've got someplace else to go on Thursday."

"Why? Is there another Lisa?"

I shook my head. "Nope. I was right: Lisa Moriarty is the one. I saw the yearbook. I look like her, way too much to be random chance. I got her married name from the school. I figure we hunt her down online this week and then go meet her." I passed him the papers from the school. He looked them over.

"What if she lives in Florida or something?"

"She doesn't. I don't know how I know, I just do."

"How did you do it?" Brody sounded amazed. He flipped through the pages.

"Come inside; it's freezing out. I'll tell you everything. When my folks come home, the story is that you brought by my homework, okay? They think I'm sick." I pulled him toward the front door. "You're going to be impressed. I swear, Wonder Woman couldn't have done a better job."

I swung open the front door and stopped short. Brody ran into my back, causing me to slide on the melted slush on the tile floor. My mom was standing in the foyer, her arms crossed over her chest. "I see you're feeling better," she said.

I swallowed, scrambling to think of something to say. "Um. What are you doing home? I didn't see your car."

"Is that the question you think is pertinent? My car is in the garage. I think the more relevant question is, why weren't you at home?"

My brain was coming up with excuses as fast as another part of my brain would reject them as bad ideas. I was going to have to lie on a much more regular basis if I planned to pull this off in the future.

"Avery and I skipped to spend the day together," Brody said. "It was my idea."

My mom and I both turned to face him. "And you are?" Mom's voice was cold and clipped.

Brody shoved his hands in his pockets. "I'm Brody, Avery's friend."

"Friend," Mom said.

I recognized her tone from when she was in court. She wasn't fooling around. "Brody and I are going out," I admitted. "There wasn't much planned for today because of the holiday, so we decided to go to his place and watch movies."

"I'm disappointed in the both of you. School isn't an optional activity."

"I convinced Avery to skip. It wasn't her idea," Brody said.

"It's not his fault," I said. I couldn't let him take the blame. I tried to tell him with my eyes that I really appreciated that he'd come up with a believable lie, but I didn't want my parents to not like him.

"I think you should go home," Mom said to Brody.

He squeezed my hand and nodded. "See you later," he said.

"I'll walk you to your car," I said. Mom opened her mouth to tell me that I'd do no such thing, but I forced myself to stand up straighter. "I'll be right back," I told her.

Brody and I stepped outside. The snow seemed to act like soundproofing. It was quiet.

"Thanks," I said.

Brody shrugged. "If I'd been smart, I would have said we spent the day working in a soup kitchen or something."

"On the upside, you didn't tell her we were out cruising for hookers and dealing drugs. That's bound to help the first impression."

"Yeah. I've got a great ability to make a good first impression on adults. She can call my mom for a reference. My mom can tell her what a screwup I am."

"You're not a screwup. You saved me back there. Trust me, she would have killed me if she knew what I'd been up to. Makes you like Batman."

He didn't laugh or smile the way he usually did at our shared joke. I leaned forward and kissed him. "You helped me. I appreciate it." He kissed me back, his mouth feeling almost hot where it touched me. He made me aware of how every inch of my body was connected to the rest. It was as if I could feel the path the sensation of his touch traveled along my nerves. "I've got to go back in," I whispered. I watched him go across the street. His car turned over slowly. I waved before going back inside.

Mom was waiting right next to the door. She turned and marched into the living room. I trailed after her. I wondered if this was how people on their way to the gallows felt. Mom pointed to the sofa, and I sank into the cushions while she walked back and forth in front of me.

"This isn't like you. Lying. Skipping school."

"I've never skipped before. Everyone skips school at least once."

Mom stopped pacing. "Are you really giving the excuse that because everyone's done it that makes it okay?"

When she put it that way, it didn't sound so good. I thought about telling her what I'd really been doing. She would have been impressed with my creativity, but I'm guessing forging being a part of the Cancer Society wasn't going to go over well. "It wasn't Brody's fault," I said. At the very least, I didn't want her to dislike him before she'd even gotten to know him.

"I know that. Unless you're saying he kidnapped you, then this was your decision. I wish you'd told us you were dating someone." She sighed. "Your dad is going to want to meet him."

"Could you not tell him about this?" I rushed to explain before she said no. "Dad will decide he doesn't like him before he's ever met him. You know how he can be. And I really like Brody. I don't want Dad to hate him."

Mom plopped down on the sofa next to me and kicked off her shoes. I could see she was tired. "I got scared when I came home to check on you and you weren't here."

"Did you think I ran off somewhere?"

"Ever since Nora died, I've been worried about you." She turned her head so we were looking at each other. "More than usual mom worry."

My throat felt tight. "I'd never hurt myself," I said.

"This is a hard time for you. I know that. Senior year, lots of changes. The pressure of getting into Duke. You and Colton breaking up. Nora dying. I wish I could make it easier, but I can't."

"I'm going to be okay," I told her.

"You're more than okay." She hugged me.

"I'm sorry I lied to you," I said, my face buried in her shoulder.

"I'm sorry I gave your new boyfriend the ice-queen welcome. We'll have to have him over during Christmas break and meet him properly."

"I'd like that."

"Now, I can't ground you without your dad asking a bunch of questions, but over the holidays you'll be volunteering to do a few extra chores around here. After Christmas we'll consider the slate clean. Deal?"

"Deal."

Mom heaved herself up from the sofa. "I'm glad we've got that cleared up. I'm putting you in charge of rustling up some pasta for dinner while I take a hot shower." She reached out and pulled me up.

"Thanks," I said.

"I don't know about you, but I feel better. I don't like when there are secrets between us."

My stomach clenched. She had no idea how many secrets were still there.

chapter twenty-four

My mom made me see Mr. Bradshaw in the morning and admit I'd lied about being sick. He looked down at his notes and shook his head sadly as if I'd confessed to having a basement full of chopped-up toddlers instead of skipping a day of classes.

"You realize you could be suspended for this," he said.

"I know." I managed to avoid rolling my eyes. No way they would suspend me for skipping once.

"Tell you what I'm going to do. I'm going to give you detention for the next two days, plus I'm going to ask you to do another ten service hours when we're back from break. Or if you're feeling you want to work it off early, you can do something in the community over the holidays, but I want a signed note verifying the hours. A suspension would be on your record and could impact your options. This way, this mistake doesn't have to have long-term implications."

The smell of his cologne was giving me a headache. "Thanks. I appreciate it."

"I trust this isn't going to happen again," he said. "I know when you're a senior it can seem like you've earned the right to blow off some steam. Get a little wild and crazy." He waved his hands in the air above his head. "Trust me, I could tell you stories about what I got up to at your age."

"No. It won't happen again." I didn't mention his wild, misspent youth. The last thing I needed was him giving me details I'd need bleach to get out of my brain.

He chuckled. "It's not that I don't like seeing more of you, but it shouldn't be under these circumstances. Next time I see you in here, I hope it's because we're celebrating some good college admission news."

I forced myself to smile. Bradshaw couldn't be creepier if he tried. There was no nice way for me to say that if I could avoid seeing him ever again, it would be just fine with me.

He shook his finger at me. "Now, don't go telling everyone I let you off easy. I'd have all of them in here asking for special treatment."

"I sure won't."

"I do have one piece of good news for you." He pointed his pen at his lap. "Want to guess what I have here?"

Ew.

Bradshaw pulled out a piece of paper from under the desk. "Duke called yesterday. They've scheduled your interview."

I wanted to lunge over his desk and grab the sheet out of his hand. "When?"

"First Monday after the holidays. Duke has an alumni member, a Ms. Fierera, who will come here to the school to meet with you. It will be about an hour." Bradshaw held out his hand. "Now, it's meant to be casual. A chance for you to tell them all about you in more detail than an application has room for. Let them get to know the real Avery. You'll also have a chance to ask any questions you have about the school. Your parents went there, so you likely don't have many, but you can ask a few strategic things."

"Like?"

"Like, are there any service clubs on campus? Something that shows you plan to give back right from the get-go, that kind of thing. If you like, we'll do a dry run tomorrow. I could meet with you during your homeroom period, put you through your paces."

"Wow. Thanks, but I'll probably practice with my parents."

Bradshaw looked depressed. If practicing college interviews with students was the highlight of his job, he should really get some career counseling and consider his other options.

I leaned forward. "Is there any way Brody and I could do our senior presentation the same day the Duke representative is here? It's really coming together, and I think it could be exactly what I need to kick my application up a notch."

"Are you sure that's not going to put too much pressure on you?"

I shook my head and tried to look calm and collected.

Bradshaw flipped open his day planner and tapped his pen on the page while he made his usual guppy face, his lips pooching in and out. "We've got a few presentations already planned for that day. I don't have you and Brody scheduled until the last week of talks. I thought you might need the extra time since you started late."

"We've been working like crazy on it. It's looking great. If we do a bit more over Christmas break, I know we can be ready."

Bradshaw's lips pursed in and out like he was kissing an imaginary friend. Fishman lives. I held my breath.

"If you feel ready, we'll make it happen. As long as you're sure. You can always discuss the project. You don't have to do a formal presentation."

"I know. I want to do the talk. I think it's going to be exactly what I need to get into Duke."

Bradshaw clapped his hands onto the desktop. "Well then, we've got a plan."

Shannon and Lydia were waiting for me in the library.

"How'd it go?" Lydia looked nervous, as if she thought

Bradshaw might have been giving me news of a terminal illness.

"It went okay. I got two detentions and extra service hours." I sat down at their table.

Shannon smiled. "Not bad. Could have been way worse."

"I also got some good news." I paused to make sure I had their full attention. "Duke's scheduled my interview."

Shannon high-fived me over the table.

"You'll ace it," Lydia said. "I'm telling you, once they meet you, they'll offer you a spot right then and there."

I wanted to believe her. This was going to be my chance. If I didn't nail the interview, I knew what would happen. I wouldn't get in. I had a good application, good grades, good volunteer experience, and a good essay. The problem was, good wasn't going to cut it. If I did a great job with the presentation, showed how I found my birth mom, it would be the kind of story that would hit home. It would make me stand out. It would take me from good to great. And I was close. Really close.

Shannon pushed me. "Stop it. I can see you obsessing right in front of my eyes."

"I know. I promise I'll stop obsessing as soon as I get in." I held up my hand like I was taking a vow. "And when that happens, I am going to throw a party like you won't believe."

"No need to wait. Karl's parents are letting him throw a holiday party this Thursday. Kick off the Christmas break with style. This way we can all get together before people take off on vacation." Shannon threw her hand over her head dramatically. "Can someone tell me why my grandparents have to live in Minnesota? Why can't they live someplace like Southern California or New York City? They're old and retired. Why are they living in the snow capital of the middle of nowhere? They could live anyplace in the world. I can't speak for all of my family, but I'd visit way more often if they lived someplace better."

"It's Christmas. It's supposed to be about family being together, not about where you're getting together," Lydia said.

"Thank you, Ghost of Christmas Future, I'll keep that in mind." Shannon tossed a piece of crumpled paper over the table at Lydia, who giggled.

"Karl's party sounds fun," I said.

"We were thinking you should invite Brody," Shannon said. She held up one perfectly painted pink fingernail to stop me from interrupting her. "Do not tell me how he's just your partner for the senior project. Do you think we didn't notice he skipped yesterday too?"

"We weren't together," I said. There was no way they would believe me, even though it was the truth.

Shannon rolled her eyes. "Whatever, Pinocchio. We all know you two have hooked up."

"Just because he's not part of our crowd doesn't mean we wouldn't like him," Lydia said. She was chewing on her lower lip, which she always did when she was anxious. "If you like him, we'll like him."

"I shouldn't have called him weird. I was out of line," Shannon said.

I pictured Karl's basement decorated for the holidays with a tree in the corner, complete with winking lights. His mom would bring down trays and trays of food and ignore the fact that the music was up so loud. The guys would huddle around the obscenely large TV screen down there, watching the sports channel while the rest of us talked about how we shouldn't eat cookies and then eat them anyway. I couldn't even picture Brody in that environment. It was great that they were making an effort, but it wasn't going to work. Brody would feel awkward, and I'd feel this huge pressure to try and make it work even though I already knew it wouldn't. There wasn't anything wrong with either set of my friends, but they didn't mix. It was like peaches and gravy: both good food items, but they shouldn't be mixed together.

"He'd love to come, but I know he's got some family thing that night. I think his dad's coming to town." The lie was out of my mouth before I even thought it through. Maybe with all the lying I was doing lately it was getting to be second nature. I reached over and gave Lydia a one-armed hug. "You guys are awesome for inviting him."

"It's true our awesomeness knows no bounds," Shannon added.

"Here's to the best Christmas ever," Lydia declared.

"Easy to say—you're not going to Minnesota," Shannon shot back.

We laughed. I felt the band of tension that seemed to follow me around loosen. Things were falling into place. Everything was going to work.

chapter twenty-five

One of the greatest tragedies in the history of mankind was the creation of the Christmas sweater. Karl's mom loved them. She was also a big fan of those sweatshirts that have the airbrushed kitten pictures on them. Karl's mom is a great cook, but she wasn't going to win any fashion awards.

"Avery!" She wrapped me in a huge hug. This year's sweater had a Santa on it with a giant Rudolph. Rudolph had a giant red stone for his nose that seemed to be exactly in the same place where her nipple would be. It made the whole thing even more odd. Karl's mom peeled my coat off as if I was in elementary school, coming in from recess.

I passed her a plate of pumpkin bread. "My mom made this for you."

"Aren't you a darling?" She hugged me again. I thought of

pointing out that I hadn't done anything other than carry the bread over, but knew it wasn't worth it. "Everyone's downstairs."

The music was loud and the room already felt too warm. Most of the basketball team had shown up, and they were in a huge debate as to exactly what was wrong with the Detroit Lions franchise and why they'd blown it again this year.

Lydia leaped up when she saw me. "You made it!"

Shannon cried out over the room, "Behold, the survivor of detention and future Duke student!"

I raised my hands in the air like a boxer after a victory and everyone let out a cheer. I wove through the crowd to the built-in bar at the back of the room. Karl's younger sister, Wendy, was serving up punch. She was a sophomore and still a bit gawky. Any coordination genes in their family had all gone to Karl. She was really smart, but she wore glasses that were that borderline between hipster and just dorky. She also tended to dress sort of frumpy, but given her mom it was amazing she had any idea what to wear. She was flushed and thrilled to be at a party with a bunch of seniors. She passed me a glass.

"Love your sweater," I said to her.

She flushed even darker and mumbled her thanks. I should talk to Lydia and have her take Wendy out for a shopping trip. With a bit of direction she could be really cute.

"Careful," Lydia warned. "There's enough sugar in that stuff to put us all in a diabetic coma."

I sipped it and then put the glass back down.

"Warned you." Lydia pushed me back a step so she could look me over. "You look great."

"New jeans," I said. It was more than that. It was that everything was clicking into place. For the first time since things fell apart I could see the light at the end of the tunnel. Brody and I were going to put the next stage of Operation Find My Birth Mom into action. Brody had told me he was going to run down another idea when I had talked to him this afternoon. He'd taken the pages I'd gotten from the school and was going to see what he could find out online. He'd wanted to get together tonight for dinner, but I'd begged off, saying Shannon, Lydia, and I had a girls' night planned.

"Hey."

I turned around and Colton was standing there. "Hey," I said back. It was clear this wasn't going to win either of us the conversationalist of the year award.

"Heard you've got the interview at Duke. Good luck with it," Colton said.

"Thanks."

We stood looking at each other, nodding. No wonder our relationship went nowhere when we were going out. We had zero to talk about. I couldn't even remember why I'd wanted to go out with him so badly last year.

"I'm glad things are, you know, good," Colton said. He fidgeted in place. A piece of his hair was curling up around his collar, and I felt a huge wave of affection for him.

I squeezed his shoulder. "You and Shannon make a great couple."

He smiled and then forced his face back into a neutral expression, trying to play it cool. Well, well, well. The mighty Colton, class president, Harvard bound, planned US senator by thirty and president by forty-five had it bad. Colton was not the type to be distracted by a crush, but it had happened. "Yeah. Shannon's great," he said. "So, see you around?"

"Sure."

As soon as he was gone from my side, Lydia slid into his place. "That looked like it went well."

"Yes. Don't think I didn't figure out that you engineered him talking to me. I swear, if the government hired you, we could fix this whole Middle East problem in weeks." I flung an arm over her shoulders. "I'm glad you talked me into coming."

Lydia smiled and waved at someone behind me. "Look who's here."

My stomach iced over. Brody was standing on the stairs, looking around the room.

"I caught him in the hall today and told him how bummed I was he couldn't come because of his dad, and he said his plans had changed." She poked me in the side. "He told me not to tell you, that he wanted to surprise you."

I swallowed and watched Brody move through the room.

"Surprise," he said.

I smiled weakly. I wished I hadn't had that punch. I wanted to throw up.

"I can't stay," he said. He smiled at Lydia. "Turns out my dad came into town after all, but since I said I was coming, I wanted to at least stop by."

"Are you sure you can't stay?" Lydia said. When he shook his head, she jumped off the barstool. "Well, I'll let you guys celebrate Avery's interview before you go." She smiled. "I know the project you guys did is going to be what gets her into Duke. She finally told us about it. I saw your pictures and they're amazing. At first I wasn't sure, but the more I heard about it the better it sounded."

I winced. Brody was staring at me. "You did the project to get into Duke. Lydia told me all about how you're pulling out all the stops to get in."

"The admissions reps are going to love it," Lydia said. "How can you go wrong? Finding Avery's birth mom, keeping a promise to a friend who's died." She shook her head as if she couldn't get over how brilliant my plan had been. "Avery, you're a genius. It's perfect."

"Sure is," Brody said. He watched her walk away.

"I can explain," I said.

"Really? Because this doesn't look like a girls' night." His eyes swept over the room stuffed with people from our class.

"I didn't want you to feel uncomfortable. I know this isn't your crowd," I said in a low voice. I peeked over my shoulder to see if people were staring at us, but everyone seemed fascinated by the game.

"Is it that you didn't want me to feel uncomfortable, or that *you* didn't want to feel uncomfortable?"

"That's not fair."

"Hiding me from your friends because you're embarrassed isn't fair. You told her I was seeing my dad." I could hear the annoyance mixed with hurt in his voice.

"It's not that. Look, come here." I dragged him into the laundry room. As soon as we pushed through the door, the volume level dropped. I ran my hands through my hair and tried to organize my thoughts. "I am not embarrassed by you. You're amazing."

"So the reason our relationship is in the witness protection program is . . . ?"

"I've told them we're dating. I'm not keeping it a secret. It's that who I am with you isn't the same as who I am when I'm with them," I explained.

"And you don't see that as a problem? That you can't be the same person? You're acting one way for your parents, another for your friends. Who are you, really?"

"I'm me," I said. My hands were balled into fists.

"And who is that, Avery?"

The door flew open and Stacey poked her head in. "Oops. Sorry. I wanted to grab some ice." She motioned at the cooler on the floor. Brody leaned over and pulled a bag out for her. "Thanks!" She ducked back out.

"I came over to give you this." Brody handed me a couple of pages. "I found your birth mom online. She has her Facebook profile left open to the public."

I stared down at the pages. "It has where she works."

"Should make finding her pretty easy for you."

"For me?"

"What? Now you're going to act like it was something we were doing together? I was so unimportant that you didn't even need to tell me why we were doing it. The whole thing was so you could get into Duke."

"That's not true." I scrambled to explain. "That was part of it, and I admit when I started, it was a big part of why I was doing this, but it's more than that now."

"Why didn't you tell me?" He slapped the side of his head. "Oh right, because the Avery you are with me doesn't even know why she's going to Duke except to make her parents happy. You might as well tell me what you think will work. What's the story again? That you wanted to make it up to Nora. Good angle. Knowing that she and I used to be friends, that was bound to get me to do what you wanted."

My eyes started to fill with tears. "Duke is what I've always wanted to do. It's what my parents expect me to do. You don't understand that."

"You're right. I don't. Course, my parents don't give a shit what I do as long as I stay out of the way."

"Don't act like you've got it all together. You don't always have to be the tortured artist," I shot back. "You say you want to be a photographer, but you don't tell anyone. Not even your parents. You don't do anything to make it happen. How can you judge me for trying to make what I want come true? We can't all wander around Europe trying to sort it out."

Brody shook his head. "You know, Nora was right about you."

His words hit me like a punch. "What does that mean?"

"I asked her once why you guys weren't friends anymore, and she said the Avery she knew didn't exist. That you were just a cutout who walked and talked and did all the right things, but might as well have been a puppet." His stare pinned me in place. "When I got to know you, I thought how sad it was that she was wrong, that she didn't know you. That you weren't like that at all. That she hadn't bothered to get to know who you were becoming. You're wrong when you say I act like I've got it together. I know I don't, but at least I'll admit it. I don't go around being whoever I think people want me to be."

My heart was in a cobralike vise, all the warmth in my body being slowly squeezed out. "I don't want to fight with you. I'm so sorry, for all of it. Everything's confused and I'm trying to sort it out."

"Well, I'll make it easier for you. You don't need to figure out where I fit in when you sort it out." He started to walk away.

I grabbed his shirt. "Don't go. Not like this. Let's go somewhere and talk."

"About what?" His voice cracked. "Is it the project? Don't worry. I won't leave you in the lurch. I'll drop off a CD with my photos on it. I'll stand up and do the presentation with you. You'll get into Duke and then you can go down there and be whoever you want."

He walked out and the door stayed open behind him, the music pulsing in like waves.

chapter twenty-six

My eyes felt like they'd been rolled in ground glass and then popped back into my head. I left the party right after Brody, making excuses that I was pretty sure no one believed. I wanted to text Brody when I got home, but I knew he wouldn't answer and that would somehow be worse. I cried, smothering the sound in my pillow so my parents wouldn't wake up. I must have slept, but it didn't feel like it. When the alarm went off, I lay in bed, staring up at the ceiling, trying to figure out if I still had the energy to do this. If I gave up trying to find her now, then everything I'd done was for nothing. I pulled out Nora's field guide and looked for inspiration.

Anything worth doing is hard. If it weren't hard, then everyone would do it. I don't know if I'll ever find my birth mom. There's every reason to believe I won't. What I know for absolute sure is that if I stop looking, then there's a 100% chance that I never will—so even if it's only a small chance, it's still a chance.

I forced myself out of bed and into the shower. I had to do this. If I quit now, then what was the point? My parents had already left for work. My mom had scribbled a note with some suggestions of things I could do around the house. I was still technically grounded as far as she was concerned. I wrote on the bottom of her note that I was going to do some Christmas shopping. That should cover me if I was late. Hopefully by the time I came home, I would have found Lisa, and that would be the important thing. I'd have to do double the chore list tomorrow to make it up. Before I could second-guess myself, I went outside, the cold air stabbing my lungs.

There weren't many cars on I-69. I pressed on the gas. Now that I'd made the decision, I wanted to be there already.

I pulled over at a gas station to double-check the directions. I stared at Lisa's profile in the printout of her Facebook page Brody had given me, my finger outlining the shape of her face. There wasn't much. She'd gone to college at Michigan State. We would have been in the same town for years. We could have passed each other on the street or in the mall. Did she know where I lived? Had she walked around looking at every baby carriage and every toddler, wondering if it was me?

I looked like her. My tenth-grade biology teacher would be relieved to know I now had proof that genetics worked. Lisa was married and had two kids. There was a photo of the whole family at the table for Thanksgiving. Her kids looked young, maybe nine and five. I swallowed. They would be my half brother and sister. I had siblings. I could hear the blood rushing in my head. I always wanted a brother or sister, and now I had one of each.

I'd searched the pages Brody had printed out, looking for some comment about how she'd had another kid and put her up for adoption, but there was nothing, although even if she liked to over-share, that might be going too far. I guessed I wanted her to have it listed so I knew it mattered. On her list of activities and interests there was nothing even remotely adoption related. She thought it was important to share with the world that she loved mystery novels and horror movies, and even what she was making for dinner most days, but she didn't seem to think the fact she had another kid merited an entry.

The important thing was that it listed where she worked. She was the education coordinator for the Beier Museum. I checked the directions from the highway one more time. I went into the grungy bathroom and caught myself in the mirror. I'd pulled on jeans and my dad's old washed-out Duke sweatshirt. Maybe I should have dressed up, but I supposed if she wasn't happy to be seeing her kid after all this time, wearing a pair of pantyhose wasn't going to make a difference. I bought a cup of coffee and a plastic-wrapped doughnut for energy and then headed back out.

It took only an hour to get to the museum, even accounting for the wrong turn off the highway. I'd wondered why the parking lot was nearly empty, until I tried the door. The place wasn't open yet and wouldn't be for another thirty minutes. I trudged back to the car. With my luck I was going to freeze to death while I waited. I could have driven around looking for someplace to go, but now that I was here, I didn't want to leave. I sipped the now-cold coffee and finished off the doughnut. It tasted like it was made out of old cotton fiber, dry and tasteless. There was an expiration date stamped on the side of the plastic, but I was afraid to look. I was willing to bet the doughnut was meant to be consumed during the previous presidential administration and had lain unclaimed on that shelf until now.

I made myself wait until the museum had been open for at least ten minutes. I thought it might look a bit odd if I was waiting outside the instant they unlocked the front door. I couldn't think they had a lot of people beating down the door, even if they did have some big special dinosaur exhibit. I didn't want to stand out. I was hoping that if I acted casual, there would be a way to spot her without announcing what I wanted.

As I locked my car, two school buses pulled into the lot, and a throng of small kids piled out. A field trip to kill time before vacation. The students all clutched bagged lunches and apparently had been consuming nonstop Red Bull shooters on the drive over; they were practically bouncing off one another. A couple of harried teachers did their best to get them into a line and marched them toward the door. They had a few high school students helping them, who were likely doing it for the volunteer hours. I picked up my pace so that I followed in behind them. I paid my fee and caught up to them in the lobby. There was a line of old Buicks along the wall with plaques telling the history of Flint. The teachers seemed too concerned with making sure the kids didn't touch or crawl into the cars to notice I had tacked myself onto their group.

"Okay, everybody! Who wants to see some dinosaurs?" The entire group of students spun around. It was Lisa, my birth mom. My breath caught. It seemed like I couldn't get enough air all of a sudden. I recognized her instantly from the photos. She was wearing khaki pants and a sweater that had a forest of pine trees around the hem. She had on dinosaur earrings and carried a giant bone in her hand. Now that she had our attention, she lowered her voice and it worked—the kids leaned in closer to hear her.

"My name is Lisa, and I'm going to show you around. We're going to travel back to what is known as the age of the reptiles, the Mesozoic era. There were three time periods in that era. Can anyone name one of them? I can give you a hint: There's a movie named after it."

"Jurassic!" a boy yelled out. He puffed up with pride when she smiled.

"That's right. The other two are the Triassic and the

Cretaceous." There was the sound of a dinosaur roar behind the closed doors, and the excitement level in the room ratcheted up a notch. Lisa clapped her hands to get their attention. "Let's go over the rules, and then we can get started."

I only half listened to her directions. She seemed natural with kids. You could tell that she actually liked them, that this wasn't a part of her job that she disliked. Our group trooped into the main part of the museum behind her. The exhibit had giant animatronic dinosaurs that would move, blink an eye, lift a foot, or toss their heads back with a giant roar. Lisa walked around the room, giving details about the various dinosaurs without ever looking at notes. My birth mom was apparently a dinosaur savant.

"Now, this one is a Brachiosaurus. He's my husband William's favorite, so I call this guy Billy." The kids snickered at the idea of giving such a huge creature such a ridiculous name. "Now, unlike my William, this guy likes eating his veggies. He's what's called an herbivore, which means he ate only plant materials. He was one of the largest dinosaurs. He would have been the size of a four-story building and weighed around fifty tons. That's the same size as six elephants!"

The triceratops was displayed so that it appeared to be captured in a pen. Lisa ducked under the wood railing and waved us closer.

"Who would like to feel this one?"

A forest of hands shot up in the air. One girl with pink and red beads strung at the end of each braid leaped into the air as if she were at a rock concert. Lisa motioned for her to come closer and let the girl rest her hand alongside the creature's chest. It heaved a breath and the girl squealed in joy.

"Okay, who else?" A line formed and each kid took their turn while Lisa explained how the mechanics of the dinosaurs worked. She looked up and met my eyes. I waited to see if there would be a flicker of recognition. I imagined that she might gasp and clutch her chest, but nothing. She didn't have any idea who I was. She beckoned me forward. "You can do it too. You're never too old."

She took my hand and pressed it to the dinosaur's hide. When she touched me, an electric shock ran up my arm, but she didn't seem to notice. The dinosaur itself was almost warm, and the skin felt like leather that had been left out in the rain and then allowed to dry. The breath felt natural, but I suppose they programmed it to feel that way. I had to remind myself that it was a fake.

"Okay, we're going to go into the other room, and then you'll have a chance to be archaeologists. We have three group workstations set up. You can either dig for bones, or do a fossil rubbing, or mix and match dinosaur parts to make your own unique dinosaur. Everyone will get a chance to try each one, so no pushing or shoving." She opened the door to the next section of the museum and the kids rushed in, jockeying for position at one of the giant interactive displays.

Uncertain of what to do now, I paused in the doorway. I noticed one of the other teen volunteers looking at me strangely. She knew I didn't belong. She crossed the room to talk to one of the teachers. I acted like I was going to go to the bathroom, but at the last moment I turned left and bolted out the door. I dashed past the startled reception clerk and out into the parking lot. I slid on a patch of black ice and fell hard onto my hands and knees. I popped up; my hands were bleeding slightly where they'd grazed the cement. My pants and sweatshirt cuffs were soaked through with the gritty slush. I looked behind me, expecting that my birth mom, or maybe the entire staff of the museum, would be racing out the door after me, but there was no one there. I stumbled into the car and peeled out.

chapter twenty-seven

I drove around. No particular destination, just up and down different streets. I'd jump on the highway, go a few exits, and then get off and drive around again. I barely noticed what I was even passing until I realized I was hungry. When I glanced at the clock, it was already late afternoon. I'd lost more time than I'd imagined. I pulled into a diner.

The inside of the restaurant looked like it was stuck in a time warp. There was a glass case at the front with pieces of pie inside that spun slowly past in a circle. The countertops were chipped laminate and the booths covered in patched teal vinyl. First I went to the bathroom and washed my hands, wincing when I patted them off with the paper towels. Once I was presentable, I slid into one of the booths and skimmed the menu. This place was not at any risk of being called a health food restaurant. A waitress went by carrying a salad. It looked like washed-out lettuce gasping its last breath with a clot of dressing squatting on top.

"You should get a Coney dog. We're known for them," my waitress said, noticing my expression as she sidled up to the table.

"Do you know how many calories are in them?" I asked.

She licked a smear of lipstick off her teeth. "Why do you think they taste so good?" She tapped her pencil on her pad. "Get the onion rings too, trust me."

I nodded and passed the menu back over to her. I looked out the window. It was starting to snow again. Sort of half sleet, half snow. The sky was a flat gray, like dull tinfoil. The waitress returned after a few minutes with a platter heaped with onion rings and a hot dog smothered in spicy Coney sauce. It tasted amazing, every greasy bite. I flipped through Nora's guide, looking for some new advice. Everything was about how to find your birth parents, but there wasn't a thing about what to do *if* you found them. I wondered what Nora thought it would be like. Was she picturing a scene where she and her birth mom ran toward each other across a giant field in slow motion? What do you do once you find her? Just tap her on the shoulder and say, *Hey, when you have a coffee break, maybe we should talk. I'm the daughter you gave up.*

I ate as slowly as I could. I didn't know what I should do next. There was a part of me that wanted to drive home and clean out the front hall closet like my mom wanted me to, but I hadn't come all this way to just look at Lisa. Saying I spotted my birth mom wasn't going to make a great presentation. I traced the Duke logo on my sweatshirt and waited for genius to strike. I wished I could call Brody and ask him for advice.

The waitress put down a refill of my soda. "Don't worry, you can stay as long as you want. They won't kick you outta here until the dinner rush. See those two over there?" She yanked her head to the side to indicate two guys playing cards at another booth. "They spend so much time here the booth is permanently molded in the shape of their asses. If the manager lets their homely bodies stick around, no way he's going to give a cute girl like you the boot. Why do you look so blue? You have a fight with your boyfriend?"

I thought about what I'd said to Brody and swallowed hard. "He's not really my boyfriend. It's not his fault. My whole life is sort of complicated these days. I'm not even upset about him. I mean, I am, but that's not all." I sighed. "Ever feel like you've screwed up everything and you're not sure what will make it better or what will make it worse?"

She nodded wisely. I suspected she saw more problems than a full-time therapist. She held up a finger and came back with a piece of pie.

"I didn't order—"

"It's on me, my favorite—strawberry. There are few things pie don't make better." She winked.

"I don't know if pie can help me," I said.

"Well, it won't make it worse." She placed the check face-down on the table next to the plate and left me alone. I closed my eyes and pictured Lisa walking around the museum. I sat straight up, banging my knees on the underside of the table. I whipped out my phone. She'd said her husband's name was William. I scrolled through the list of people with her married name in the phone book. There was only one William. I chewed on my lower lip. It wouldn't hurt to look. I checked Google Maps. Her house wasn't that far away. She might be home from work soon. The museum closed at four thirty. My heart started beating faster. Going to the museum had been a mistake. I realized this now. It wasn't fair for me to expect her to recognize me, and even if she had, what did I think she could do about it in the middle of her workday?

I parked three or four houses away from hers and hunched down in my seat far enough to look casual, but not so far down I'd look like some weirdo. The neighborhood was full of well-kept older houses. You could tell it was made up mostly of families. There were a lot of minivans with their "my kid is on the honor roll" bumper stickers, and swing sets in the yards. Her house had a half-melted snowman on the front lawn. There hadn't been enough snow to make a proper one, so he looked almost more mud and grass than snow, but someone hadn't been able to wait. This was stupid. I had no idea what she might get up to after work. There was no reason to assume she would come straight home, and even if she did, I wasn't sure what I would say. It was then that she pulled into the drive, the garage door opening before her like magic.

I gave her a few moments to get settled and then walked up to the front door. She had her Christmas lights strung around the windows. I wondered if she was the kind of person who got all excited about the holidays, or if these were still up from the year before. I rang the bell. Inside I could hear the bark of a dog and a voice telling someone to turn the TV down.

Lisa flung open the door and looked at me. I could tell she was trying to process what I was doing there. "Aren't you the volunteer from the school visit today?"

I nodded.

"What are you doing here?" She looked past me to see if I was alone. Maybe she expected a school bus full of kids wanting to know more about dinosaurs to be parked in the driveway.

"I'm Avery," I said.

She scrunched up her face in confusion for a moment. Then it clicked into place for her. She understood. She took a step back as if she thought I might lunge at her. Or maybe she was simply shocked that I didn't have the cone head from my baby picture.

"I wanted to find you—" I got out before she grabbed my hand.

"We can't talk here." She pulled me behind her into the yard and then into the open garage. She kept glancing around as if snipers might be sneaking up on us, or more likely that the neighbors might have noticed. "What do you want?"

"I wanted to meet you," I said.

"So you just show up at my house?" She pinched the bridge of her nose. "My kids are inside."

"I didn't plan this very well," I admitted. "There's been so much going on lately, I thought meeting you would help me . . . I don't know, sort it out. Make sense of things."

"How did you find me?"

"I guess I channeled my inner Nancy Drew." I gave a nervous laugh, but she didn't join me. So much for impressing her right off the bat. "I had some information about you from the adoption. That led me to your old high school." I decided not to mention lying to get her current information from the school; we already weren't off to a great start. "Plus, there's a lot of stuff online these days." I shrugged. "It wasn't that hard."

She barked out a laugh. "Here I tell the kids to watch what they put on the Internet. Guess I should take my own advice."

My guts felt hollowed out. I hadn't expected her to weep and fling her arms around me, but I didn't think it would go like this. "I thought maybe you kept your profile open because you were hoping that I was looking for you."

"Hang on." She went over to a metal shelving unit against the wall and pushed aside some bulk containers of granola bars and juice boxes, then pulled out a crumpled pack of cigarettes. "I quit a few years ago, but I keep some around for emergencies.

I'm thinking this counts." She flicked the lighter and took a deep drag, then blew the smoke up into the rafters. "You don't smoke, do you?"

"No."

"Good. Bad habit." She took another deep drag. "I know I'm probably doing this all wrong. I thought if I ever heard from you it would be a letter or something. I didn't really imagine you showing up here. You're not in trouble, are you? Things with your family are okay?"

I crossed my arms over my chest. "Things with them are fine. It's nothing like that."

She looked relieved. "You're seventeen now. A year older than me when I had you. Can you imagine that? Having a baby?"

I shook my head.

"When I realized I was pregnant, it seemed like my entire world was crashing in. My parents were crushed. Every time my mom looked at me, she'd start crying. I could tell my dad was sick about the whole thing. Mentally, I was still his little girl. The idea that I was having sex freaked him out. I thought I was so old, mature. Now that I have my kids, I realize just how young I really was."

I noticed that she talked about her kids as if I was completely unconnected to them. As if I wasn't her child too.

"I wanted you to have the best life possible, and there was no chance I could do that. Your parents seemed perfect. I read their bios and thought, who wouldn't want them as a family? They were the kind of parents I would have picked for myself if I could have. I want you to know how important to me it was that you have a good home."

"They're good parents. It isn't that they did something wrong, it's just that something is missing for me. I wanted to fill in the gaps. I'm not asking you to step up and be my mom. I just want to know you. I thought you'd want to know me, too."

She took one last puff of her cigarette and then ground it under her heel. "I chose adoption because I wanted you to have a good life, but I also wanted a fresh start for me."

"Is that why you stopped writing? You wanted to start over?"

She flinched. "It sounds bad. I did what I thought was the right thing for you, but then I decided I had to do the right thing for me." She seemed to avoid my eyes.

"What does that mean?" I hated how my voice sounded so needy. I wanted to come across as someone worth listening to, but I was failing. No wonder she didn't want me around.

She sighed. "It means I deserved a fresh start too. I didn't want to be the twenty-year-old who already had a baby. I wanted to be like everyone else. I was in college and dating and didn't want to drag my past mistakes into my future."

I winced—that was me, her past mistake. "I'm not trying to cause problems for you. It's hard for me to explain everything, but I wanted to find you, partly because of this school project, but it turned into so much more. It would really help me if you—"

She cut me off. "Don't you understand? My husband knows nothing about you. I never told him I had a baby before I met him. I can't tell him now: *Oh hey, by the way, I have a seventeen-year-old daughter I never mentioned.* How do I explain you to my kids?" She stopped suddenly and pressed her fingers to her temples. "And if I don't tell them who you are, what are we supposed to do? Sneak around? Meet on the sly?" She looked afraid.

I stared at her. I hadn't expected that she was living every day thinking about me, but it never occurred to me that she'd made a whole life without letting anyone else know I even existed. "You don't want anything to do with me." My voice came out flat and unemotional.

She shook her head, her eyes filling with tears. "It's not that simple. I don't know. I'm not trying to hurt you, but you can't expect to show up here and have everything be fine. I can't make this decision now." Her face was flushed, and she was spinning her wedding ring around her finger. "You should go. This isn't the time or place for this. I need some time to think, to figure out—" She looked around. "It's almost Christmas. I can't tell my family now."

I knew she wanted to come across as firm, but I could tell she was scared. She was afraid of me. I was like a ticking time bomb in her house. A suicide bomber. Boom. I could blow up her family just like that. "Do you want my number so we can talk about it later?" I pulled my bag open to get some paper out, but she waved my hand away like she was afraid to touch me.

"I can reach you through the adoption service."

I stared at her. That was it? Don't call me, I'll call you? I considered trying to explain the issue with Duke and that looking for her had cost me Brody, and that I needed her help now, but I could tell it wouldn't make a difference. She had her own family to worry about and I wasn't a part of it. My shoulders slumped. As I walked down the drive, I heard the door from the garage to the house open.

"Mommy, who are you talking to?"

"No one, baby."

chapter twenty-eight

It snowed on the drive home. Big, fat, mutant flakes. The kind that look like giant cotton balls falling from the sky. It was a holiday postcard, with the fresh snow the finishing touch. People had their colored lights on, and some had gone way over the top with full Nativity scenes, giant inflatable Santas popping out of chimneys, or dancing penguins. As I pulled into my neighborhood, there was a group of kids having a snowball fight. It seemed wrong that the holiday was going on for everyone else. My world had exploded, but it didn't make the slightest dent for anyone else.

My mom was home. She'd already changed out of her work clothes and was making a batch of her famous peppermint snowball cookies. She whacked a Ziplock bag full of candy canes with a rolling pin, crushing them so she could sprinkle them on top of the batch she'd just taken out of the oven.

"Hey, honey!" She smiled. "Guess who is off work for the next full week? I'm thinking we go on a cookie-making spree for the next few days. You in?"

I tried to summon some excitement for her plan. "Sure."

"Your friend Brody stopped by this afternoon."

My mouth dried up. "What'd he say?"

"Not much." She motioned to the corner of the counter. "He dropped off a CD for your project. He said you knew he was going to bring it by."

I picked up the case and turned it over in my hands.

"Did you find what you were looking for today?" Mom asked.

I looked up quickly. "What do you mean?"

Her eyebrows went up at my tone. "You said in your note you were doing some Christmas shopping."

"Oh. Right." I swallowed hard. I was going to start crying. "Nope. I didn't find it."

Mom came around the kitchen island, wiping her hands on the kitchen towel. "What's wrong?"

"Nothing."

She took me by my elbows and twisted my body so we were facing each other. "You've always been a sensitive person, but I refuse to believe you're this upset by shopping. What's going on?"

I swallowed again. I couldn't meet her eyes. "I found Lisa," I whispered.

Mom let out a low breath. "Okay. This is a sit-down conversation." She led me over to the sofa and we sat side by side. "Start at the beginning."

I explained how Brody and I had figured out who she was and how I'd gone to the school to get her address. "Are you mad?"

She shook her head. "I'll admit, I'm impressed. I've seen lawyers with less creativity in the research department. I shouldn't have closed the door when you told me you were looking for her. Then we could have talked about this. You shouldn't have had to go by yourself today."

"She's married now and has other kids. She never told her husband about me." My lower lip was shaking. "She's ashamed of me."

Mom pulled my face up so she could see me. "She is not ashamed of you. She doesn't know you. She's ashamed of what she thinks people will think of her. There's nothing about you that is shameful."

"It doesn't feel like that." A tear fell from my eye and dropped onto my jeans, leaving a perfect dark blue circle.

"Is this about Nora?"

"Partly," I admitted. "I wasn't a good friend to her. Not as good as I could have been." The words felt like explosive grenades that I'd thrown into the middle of the room.

"Nora let herself down." Mom squeezed my hand.

I picked at the hem of my sweater. "But I wasn't there for

her. She thought I'd changed, that I wasn't who I used to be, and she was right. I found her embarrassing sometimes. I didn't want her to mess up my life. Ironic, isn't it? Maybe meeting Lisa is the universe's way of teaching me a lesson."

"I'm not sure the universe took time out of its busy schedule for that." She tapped my wrist. "I'm not saying that there isn't something you can learn and take away from what happened with Nora, but you also have to accept that Nora was a complex, complicated girl. You can't expect perfection from her or yourself."

"I feel pretty far from perfect these days. I lied to Brody." I swallowed. "I didn't think he'd want to help me if he knew it was about getting into Duke. That's why I started all of this. I wanted to get into Duke so bad, and all of a sudden this seemed like the ideal answer. I told him what I knew would convince him to help me. What's everyone going to think if I don't get in? They'll all shake their heads and feel bad for me. 'Poor Avery, she didn't quite measure up.' If I don't get in, what else can I do?"

Mom shrugged. "Go somewhere else." She patted my knee. "Part of life is dealing with what happens and trusting that things happen for a reason."

Easy for her to say. She'd gotten into Duke with no trouble.

"No one gets what they want all the time," she said, reading my mind. "I always wanted a baby, to be a mom. It wasn't something that I thought I needed to plan; I just assumed it would happen. After your dad and I got married, I figured

I'd get pregnant right away. When it didn't happen, I didn't panic. I figured it was just a problem that had to be solved, and I prided myself that problem solving was something I did really well. I read up on what foods I should be eating. How to time things so we were trying on the best possible dates. I went to see my doctor and did every test modern medicine could dream up. I made your dad stop riding his bike. I rearranged our bed so it was in line with feng shui principles in case that made a difference."

"Really?" My mom usually made fun of that kind of thing.

"Ask your dad about it sometime. He broke his toe one night coming to bed because I'd moved the dresser. He couldn't wear shoes for a couple of weeks. He had to wear slippers to work."

I almost laughed, picturing my dad hobbling around his office in giant fuzzy slippers.

"When everything I tried still didn't make a difference, I got upset. More than upset—mad. Every time someone would tell me that it was sure to happen as soon as I stopped worrying about it I wanted to smack them. I'd see all these people who were pregnant who didn't want to be, and I wondered why it was so easy for them and so hard for me. How could I pray for something like that and not have my prayers granted? I wasn't praying for money or a job, but for a chance to have a baby. I even went to a psychic."

My mouth fell open. My mom was really not the psychic type. "Why?"

"I thought maybe she could tell me what I'd done wrong. Maybe I'd tortured kittens in a previous life or something. Maybe my chakras, or whatever, were off. I would have done anything to get pregnant. Talked to anyone. Done any strange thing that I thought would work. That's when your grandma asked me something important. She asked me if it was about being pregnant or about being a mom."

"So you decided to adopt."

"Yep. Your dad and I went to see someone that same week to start the process. A little over a year later we brought you home. The instant I looked at you, I knew you were mine. More than if you'd been born from my body. Getting pregnant is biology, but the fact that out of the whole world we came together was about destiny. I loved you from the moment I heard of you, and the second I held you I knew you were my daughter. You were always meant to be my daughter. You can't make things happen in life. You can only move toward what you want and have faith that life will lead you to what is meant to be. If I'd kept trying to do it my way, I wouldn't have you."

My throat felt full and tight. She smiled, and I threw myself into her arms and we held on to each other. She rubbed my back in small circles, the way she had when I was small. I felt myself unwind. The tight band that had been around my chest since I'd walked away from Lisa melted away. "So, do I stop trying to get into Duke?"

Mom laughed. "Of course not. Not if you really want to

go. Our family is known for being annoyingly focused. I'd blame your dad, but I do the same thing. You didn't stand a chance. You were doomed from the start to be stubborn. You work your butt off to get in, but you remember that if it doesn't happen, then you're going to be okay. Getting into Duke isn't about what other people think of you, it's about what it lets you do."

I sat quietly, thinking about what she said. "The whole focus of my project is wrong."

"Lucky for you, you've got a couple of weeks off to work on it." Mom smiled. "I can keep your energy up with a nonstop flood of Christmas cookies. Never underestimate the power of candy canes."

I felt a flicker of excitement. Ideas started to rattle around in my head. I pictured the photos that Brody had done. They'd still work. "Brody's mad at me."

"Do you think he has a reason to be?"

I nodded. "I let him down."

"That's the hard thing with some people. They see us not just for who we are, but for who we could be. They hold us to a higher standard. They make us better because they believe we can be better, and that makes us believe it too."

In that moment I began to believe.

chapter twenty-nine

They were calling it Snowmageddon. The news anchors were practically giddy as they predicted that we could get up to three feet overnight. They'd already forced the weatherman to do his segment while standing outside with the wind nearly blowing him over and the snow pelting him in the face. They always stick the weatherpeople in the shitty weather, as if you couldn't imagine how bad it was unless you saw someone standing in it. Being a weatherperson ranked pretty high on the "shitty jobs I don't ever want to do" list. Right around being a spa aesthetician who does bikini waxes on other women all day. Some things can't be unseen.

The police had issued a warning that if you didn't have to be out on the roads, you should stay in. Places all across town closed early and canceled their New Year's Eve parties. I'd talked to Lydia and Shannon earlier in the day. Shannon felt the storm was out to ruin her life. She'd found an amazing dress to wear, and the idea of sitting around with her parents and younger brother watching movies instead of going out dancing wasn't her idea of a perfect way to ring in the New Year. I acted as if I was equally annoyed about the storm—*how dare Mother Nature ruin our last New Year's as high schoolers.* The truth was I didn't mind staying home.

I've always loved New Year's Eve. Some people are crazy about Halloween or Christmas, and even Fourth of July has its big fans, but for me there's something appealing about the idea of a new year. It feels like anything is possible as long as you put it on your resolution list. Life gives you a do-over.

I'd spent the bulk of the Christmas break working on the project. I tried to revise what I had, but in the end I knew I had to chuck everything other than Brody's photos. It was easier once I stopped trying to fix things and started over. I laid out the presentation and spent hours trying to figure out if I had the slides in the perfect order. I gave the presentation to myself in my bedroom mirror. I practiced lines from the talk in the shower and wandered around the house mumbling to myself. This morning my dad had come into my room and taken my laptop away. He declared that the next two days were project free. At first I was annoyed with him, but he was right. I was getting obsessed. Now that the project was done and I couldn't do anything else, I just wanted it to be over.

I stared out the window. The cars parked outside were already buried under a layer of snow. I could still make out their shapes, but if we got much more snow, they'd disappear. I hoped they had the plows out already. School wasn't due to start for a couple of days, but if we had a snow day, I was pretty sure I would snap. I was prepared to go out with a shovel and dig the city out myself.

"Come down soon!" my dad cried out. "The countdown is starting in a few minutes."

"Okay," I called back.

I pulled out Nora's notebook. I wondered what her mom was doing tonight. I could picture her getting up to get something from the fridge and coming across Nora's chipped Mickey Mouse mug in the cupboard. Her house would be full of these Nora land mines, things that would blow up in her face and remind her all over again that Nora was gone. This was the beginning of a new year that Nora would never know.

"Do you wish you hadn't done it?" I said softly. I didn't expect her to answer. I wanted to believe that after we died we went to a fluffy cloud in heaven and could look down and watch things on earth like it was a TV show. If life were like a book, she'd become a sarcastic sidekick ghost that would follow me around, offering helpful advice as I moved through life. But life isn't a book. Nora didn't get a chance to realize that what she did was a mistake. She bailed and left the rest of us to cope with it.

I'd never be able to make it right with Nora. I'd never be able to apologize. What was broken between us would stay broken for my entire life. There would be no picture of us at graduation with our arms around each other. Nora would never go to college, or travel through Europe, or learn Thai cooking. She'd never sort out what she wanted to do for a job. She'd never get married or have her own kids, or skip getting married and move to Paris to be an artist. She was out of choices.

I ran my hand over the notebook one more time. "I'm sorry. You were right. I wasn't being myself. I don't think I knew who I was. I'm still not sure, but I promise I won't stop trying to figure it out."

I stood and pulled a box off the top shelf of my closet. My mom had started the box for me when I was little. She'd tucked away various things. The candle off my first birthday cake, a selection of homework assignments from over the years, the small stuffed bunny that had been my best friend for years. I'd added to the box. There was a red hair ribbon that I'd stolen from Walmart and then had always felt too guilty about to wear. I had my first-year cheer pin and a medal from eighth grade when I ran track. I had a pressed rose that Colton had given me. I dug through the box until I found the picture I'd made in first grade of me as a teacher in the future. I wished I could have had Nora's picture of her as a mermaid. I tucked Nora's notebook inside the box and slid it back onto the shelf. I didn't need it anymore.

I wasn't able to make it right with Nora, but I could do all the things she couldn't. I owed her that, to do as much as possible with the time I had that she'd given away.

"The ball's going to drop!" Dad yelled out.

I ran down the stairs and joined my parents in the living room. My mom passed me a glass of champagne. I almost dropped it in surprise.

"This is not a regular thing. It's New Year's," Dad said with his stern face.

"So, you're saying it's not okay for me to swill down your vodka?" I asked in mock surprise.

"Ten! Nine!" Mom said, pointing toward the TV. The shot was of Times Square with crowds of people all jostling forward to be as close as possible to the front. The ball started to slide down. We joined the countdown as if we were part of the party.

"Three, two, one!" we yelled out in unison.

My dad leaned over and kissed my mom and then my cheek. I hugged them both. I tipped back the glass of champagne. The fizz tickled the back of my throat.

My phone on the table started to buzz.

"Ah, the troops are checking in," Dad said.

I grabbed the phone. There was a text from Shannon. *HAPPY NY! BEST YEAR EVR!* Lydia had sent a photo of her smiling at the camera in one of those goofy, paper New Year's hats with a black feather sticking up. I texted them back. I put the phone down and then picked it up. No guts, no glory. I'd blame the champagne if it turned out badly.

HAPPY NEW YEAR I texted to Brody. I held the phone, willing it to vibrate with a message, but nothing.

chapter thirty

D on't be nervous," Lydia said. She was bouncing on the balls of her feet. "Apparently, the secret is to pretend everyone's in their underwear and to bend at the knees a bit so you don't feel like passing out."

Shannon rolled her eyes. "Stop talking about it. You're making me nervous and I'm not doing anything."

"I'm trying to help!" Lydia said. "Oh, and don't drink too much water. You don't want to have to pee in the middle of your talk. There's nothing worse than having to pee when you can't."

"Nothing?" Shannon asked. "What about cancer? Cancer seems worse. Or being bitten by a shark, that would suck worse."

"Zombies," I added.

"Zombies would be totally worse," Shannon said. "Or what about that flesh-eating bacteria?"

"Ha, ha, ha," Lydia said. "You two could do stand-up comedy."

I squeezed her. "You're the best. I appreciate your help."

"We'll sit near the front so you can see us," Shannon said. "We'll be cheering you on. We'll start the crowd doing the wave. After all, we're professionals."

"Thanks, guys." I pulled on the silver chain I was wearing. It was my mom's lucky locket. She wore it every time she had to appear in court. She'd lent it to me this morning.

"There's the lady of the hour!" Bradshaw brayed out.

"Does he lube his lips, or are they that oily all the time?" Shannon said softly.

Bradshaw wove through the crowds in the hall. I realized who must be with him and forced myself to stand up straighter. I held out my hand when she got close. My dad and I had practiced shaking hands over the weekend. He was a big believer that people judged others by their handshake. *Never be limp. No one trusts someone with a limp hand.* I shook her hand, hoping I'd found the sweet spot between hand crushing and dead fish.

"I'm Ms. Fierera," she said. She was tall and curvy. "I'm looking forward to our interview."

"Me too," I said.

"Well, let's get this show on the road." Bradshaw pointed us toward the auditorium. "I think you'll be impressed at the level of the presentations, Ms. Fierera. I like to think I've guided some fine young minds toward their futures."

"I'm sure," she said, her voice neutral.

"It's such a special thing to impact young lives," Bradshaw said as he took her elbow.

"Poor woman." Lydia watched her walk away. "I hope Duke gave her hazard pay for having to put up with Bradshaw. She could die of asphyxiation from his cologne."

"You ready?"

I turned around and Brody was standing there. He looked uncomfortable in a pair of pressed khaki pants and a sweater. "You dressed up," I said.

He looked down at himself. "Yeah. I thought I should. You look good."

"Thanks." I realized I was biting my lip and made myself stop.

"We should have practiced this," Brody said. He shifted from foot to foot.

If he was nervous now, there was nothing to be gained by telling him I'd changed everything from our first draft. "Don't worry. I practiced enough for both of us. I just need you to run the projector and move the slides forward."

"Okay, you guys, break a leg," Lydia said. She gave me a hug and then quickly leaned over and hugged Brody. He froze and then managed a hug back.

"Are you ready for this?" I asked Brody after they walked away. I wanted to apologize, but I knew sorry wasn't going to be good enough.

He shrugged. "You're doing all the hard stuff."

"Your pictures are perfect."

I could hear applause coming from the auditorium. Someone must be finishing up their talk.

"You'll do great," Brody said.

"I don't know, but I'm going to do my best."

I was afraid when I stood on the stage I might lock up and not be able to say anything, but I didn't. I looked out over the crowd. Bradshaw and Ms. Fierera were near the middle of the audience, sitting on the aisle. As promised, Shannon and Lydia were in the front row. Colton was sitting next to Shannon, and he gave me a thumbs-up. I looked around. I didn't know what the person I was looking for looked like. I'd have to begin and see what happened. I nodded at Brody and he clicked on the first slide. I cleared my throat and spoke.

"My first talk was going to be on school reform." My voice sounded really loud over the microphone. "I didn't pick the topic because I really have an interest in it. I picked it because I thought it sounded important. Like something that would impress people. I don't know much about school reform, but I do know a lot about trying to impress people. I've spent a lot of time making sure that I gave the right impression and hiding anything that I didn't feel lived up to the expectations people might have.

"Then my friend Nora died earlier this year. She was doing her talk on her quest to find her birth mom. I decided I'd make finding my mom my new topic. You can't get more impressive than that, helping a deceased friend complete a quest. This entire talk was going to be about the importance of family and how by finishing Nora's project I'd done something in her memory. That was a lie. I was doing it because I thought it made me look good. I know that sounds bad, and I deserve it. This project isn't about any of those things anymore."

Brody was staring at me as he mouthed, "What are you doing?" I ignored his question and nodded at the projector to remind him of his job. He clicked the next slide over.

"Before I go too far, I have to thank my partner, Brody. The photos you see are his. And they're amazing, so if you could let him know, that would be great."

The crowd let out a whoop. A woman who had been standing at the side clapped. It had to be her. I couldn't tell if she was impressed or doing what she thought was polite. Brody jumped when he saw her. He hadn't known I'd invited his mom. It was time she saw for herself how amazing he was.

Brody was trying to catch my eye, but I didn't look at him and instead kept going. All the practice was paying off.

"Friends are a kind of family. A family of choice." I pointed at Brody. He paused for a second and then clicked forward, showing more of his pictures. "I was friends with Nora for years." Here I'd inserted some pictures from home of Nora and me as kids. Brody was blinking madly as they went by. I wasn't sure, but I thought he might be trying not to cry. "We grew apart. That happens. But it was more than that. I didn't try and stay in touch, because I didn't feel like she fit in. I didn't realize that there is always room for more people in your life who care for you. You don't 'fit in' friends. You make room for them. I let her down as a friend and I will always be sorry for that."

I rattled off some of the research I'd dug up about the importance of friendship, with Brody whizzing through the slides that detailed things in tables and graphs. I showed that people with good solid friendships lived longer and were less likely to have a whole range of diseases. Those who did become ill recovered faster if they felt supported by their friends. I didn't have to look at my notes once.

"One thing I've learned in this process is not to take my friends for granted. That I need them and that I can be who I am with them." I smiled down at Shannon and Lydia. I cleared my throat and motioned for Brody to click forward again.

"Part of this project was also the search for my birth mom." I rattled off more statistics on adoption rates. "I thought if I found my birth mom, not only would it make for a great project, but it would somehow help me figure out who I was. I wanted to impress the people at Duke. There was a lot riding on finding her. Brody and I found her." I flashed a slide that showed the various resources available for adoptees. "My birth mom lives not far from here. She's married now with more kids. I had a chance to meet her over the holiday." I could see Brody was holding his breath. I knew he'd suspected I'd gone to meet her, but I hadn't told him what happened. I'd considered putting in a picture of Lisa, but that didn't seem fair to her, so I'd left it out. It wasn't really about her. "If this project was really impressive, then I'd point to the back of the room and have her come in here. Then we could hug in front of everyone." A few people in the audience turned around to see if she was walking down the aisle. Bradshaw was one of them, but Ms. Fierera kept her eyes on me.

"She didn't want anything to do with me." I heard someone in the audience let out a low whistle of shock. "She might change her mind in the future. She might not. What I realized is that it didn't matter. My parents adopted me. They've never seen me as their adopted daughter. Only their daughter. The idea that meeting someone would fill in the gaps was the wrong way to look at the picture. I'm responsible for filling in those gaps myself. I have to figure out who I am, maybe with a bit of help from my friends. It's okay that I don't know all the answers now, but it's not okay to expect other people to fill them in for me.

"I wanted to impress people. I worried about what people might think of me, but I didn't worry enough about who I really was and who I was becoming." I looked at Brody. "I let people down. I let down people who mattered because I was afraid if I was honest, maybe they wouldn't like me." My voice caught and I paused to pull myself together.

Brody clicked to the last slide. It was his photo of the little girl sitting on the log. I told the story to the audience about how when I'd seen the picture, I thought it looked almost eerie and how Brody had told me the truth behind the shot. "I realize now that you can't control how people see things. Everyone brings their own perspective. I've learned that the only thing I can control is myself. I found my birth mom, but it didn't matter. What I really needed to find was myself. I'm not there yet, but I'm getting closer." I took a deep breath. It was over. "Thanks for your attention."

The audience applauded. Shannon and Lydia stood up, trying for a standing ovation, which made me smile. I could see the next two people standing off to the side, ready to do their talk, so I paused to look one last time around the auditorium and then walked off the stage.

chapter thirty-one

Once I was in the wings, my legs started to shake, and I sat down on a roll of carpet left behind from the fall drama production. I felt light-headed. Brody wove his way through the abandoned set pieces and sat next to me.

"That was some talk," he said.

"Sorry I didn't tell you I changed it. I felt like it was something I had to do myself." I glanced over. "You're not mad about me calling your mom, are you?"

Brody shook his head. "No. I can't believe she came."

"It seemed like she wanted to come. I think she was just waiting to be invited. I'm sorry about all of it, the way I acted."

"Me too. You were right, you know, when you said I was acting like a tortured artist." He pretended to stab himself in the heart. "I got on your case because you were trying to make things happen in your life, when I was too afraid to admit what I wanted in case someone told me I couldn't have it."

"Your parents should know you're an amazing photographer. I didn't know your dad's number, so I had to settle for just your mom."

"I'm not sure it will make a difference. She sort of sees what she wants to see. I suppose I shouldn't let it get to me so much."

"I think your parents don't know you. That's their fault, but you could try harder."

"Forget about my parents. I should have tried harder to understand what you were going through. I didn't get why finding your birth mom mattered so much to you and Nora."

"It's hard to explain. You know where you come from; knowing that history matters. People talk about how they have Irish heritage, or have a temper like their dad, or they're proud of great-grandparents who had the guts to immigrate for a better life. They want to be in the army because they had some relative who did that, or people talk about how they're artistic like Great-Aunt Harriet. I have none of that history to build on. I think I thought if I could know those things I'd somehow know myself better."

"Having that history isn't always a good thing either," he pointed out. "Look at my family."

"You're who you want to be."

Brody was quiet for a beat. "It's weird. History can hold you back if you let it."

"I think I was afraid of my history. Really, when you peel everything back, the truth was that I was abandoned. My birth mom didn't want me, so she just walked away. I always said that didn't bother me, but it did. I think I was always trying to make sure that it never happened again. If I could be perfect enough, no one else would leave."

Brody pulled me closer to him. "But you've got it all wrong. You weren't abandoned."

I cocked an eyebrow at him. "What would you call it?"

"You were lost so you could be found." He leaned forward so our faces were just a few inches apart. "She made sure you had a family. She left you to be discovered."

I sat and thought about his words. "What if there's nothing to be discovered?"

Brody smiled. "There's a whole world to explore."

I leaned forward and then hesitated. Brody met me the rest of the way and we were kissing.

He pulled back after a minute and smiled at me. "You know, the two of us are pretty messed up."

"Candidates for years of therapy."

"Now, you know what Bradshaw would say." Brody made the fish mouth. "Our tortured pasts are what will make us the best superheroes. Batman had to suffer, after all, in order to really embrace his bat side."

"What about Wonder Woman? I don't think she had a tortured past. She was an Amazon princess. No sign of issues.

It seems to me, you and Batman are the messed-up ones."

Brody scoffed. "Are you kidding me? The woman has an invisible plane and likes to fight using a Lasso of Truth. That's a girl with some issues. When you want to tie people up in order to talk to them—you have problems. Who knows what happened to her in the Amazon? You know what they say: What happens in the Amazon stays in the Amazon."

"Do you want to go out this weekend with my friends? They want to get to know you," I said.

"Can you risk it?" Brody smirked. "I mean, I'm pretty hot. Now they've seen my pictures, and it's just a matter of time until they find out about my Batman alter ego. Chicks dig a guy with a tortured past."

"I'll risk it. Besides, if you get out of line, I'll tie you up with my lasso."

Brody winked. "Now, that sounds interesting."

I pushed him in the side, but then leaned forward and kissed him again. He put his arms around me, pulling me even closer. I folded into him. The place where our mouths met was the only real thing that anchored me to the earth, otherwise I'd float away.

Someone behind us cleared her throat and we flew apart. Ms. Fierera was standing there. She looked like she was trying not to smile. I stood in a hurry and nearly tripped over the carpet roll. I would have fallen except for the fact Brody caught my elbow and kept me from going down. I pulled my skirt into place. Great. Now she could add "uncoordinated" to my file.

"Sorry to disturb you," Ms. Fierera said. "I wondered if you'd like to do your interview now."

I tucked my hair behind my ears. "Yes, that would be great."

"Your guidance counselor has arranged for us to use his office so we can have some privacy." She smiled at me. "I'll meet you there in ten minutes."

I nodded.

She started to walk away and then stopped and turned back around. "You may not have been trying to do it, but for the record, Ms. Scott, you were impressive out there. Very impressive."

When she was gone, Brody picked me up and spun me around. "She loves you."

I whacked him on the back so he'd put me down "Let's not get carried away. I haven't blown it yet. There's still time."

"No way. I could see it in her eyes. Trust me, Batman knows these things." He smiled. "She's from Duke—she's gotta be smart, right? She'd be crazy not to love you."

"Maybe."

"I do."

I stared at Brody; maybe I wasn't understanding what he meant. "You do . . . what?"

He winked and then kissed me. "Knock her dead."

chapter thirty-two

The sun was out and the sky was a perfect flat blue. The snow was blindingly white outside. The weather, combined with the fact it was a Friday, meant no one was interested in focusing on school.

"Okay, people, pay attention! The way you fill out the form is how your name is going to appear on your diploma in the spring. You need to decide if you want your middle name on there. No nicknames!" Bradshaw waved his hands around, trying to keep our attention.

The entire senior class was in the cafeteria so that we could go over details for graduation. We were all given copies of our transcripts and the list of what courses we had in the spring semester so we could each double-check our credits. We filled out forms to order caps and gowns. There was also an opportunity to choose a selection of overpriced Northside High paraphernalia, including class rings that no one would be interested in ten minutes after graduation.

I spotted Brody a few tables over and he smiled.

"He's got it bad for you," Lydia said, noticing his gaze.

I flushed. "It's mutual."

"You know, I was looking at a map the other day. New York and Durham aren't that far apart. You could drive it in a day." Lydia acted like she was interested in her form, but I could see her smiling.

"Looking out for me, huh?"

She jostled me with her elbow. "What are friends for?"

I still hadn't heard anything from Lisa, my birth mom. I didn't know if that was because she was trying to decide how to fit me into her current life, or if she'd made the decision that there wasn't any room. I'd hoped there would be a typical Hollywood ending where she would show up and confess that she'd made a horrible mistake, but it hadn't happened yet. I was trying to wrap my head around the idea that it might not. As my parents, my real parents, pointed out, if she didn't take the time to know me, it would be her loss. I was working on convincing myself of that and in the meantime taking some comfort in the idea that my parents believed it completely. She wasn't the birth mom I wanted, but when it really mattered, she'd done the right thing. She made the decision to give me the family I needed.

Bradshaw clapped his hands to get our attention. "We're

going to do one more thing. Take out a sheet of paper." He walked up and down the rows, passing out plain envelopes. "You're going to write a letter to your future self and put it in the envelope. I'll collect them all and box them up. For your ten-year reunion you'll get your letter back." People shifted in their chairs, pulling out pens and cracking jokes about what they were going to write. Ten years from now seemed like a lifetime. We'd be twenty-eight, which seemed impossibly old.

"You're the only one who will see the letters, so feel free to be open and honest. Talk about what you hope you've accomplished in that time, your hopes and dreams. When you're done with your letter, seal it up and give it to me. Once you've done that, then you're free to go back to class."

I rubbed the silver locket my parents had given me for nailing my interview with Duke. I'd heard two weeks ago that I'd been accepted. My mom declared that everyone needed their own lucky locket. My pen glided across the page.

Dear Future Me,
It's hard to imagine you/me in the future. We're supposed
to write what we hope for—I guess so in the future we can
either laugh at what dorks we were in high school, or get
depressed over all the things we wanted to do and never did.

My wishes for the future are pretty vague. I used to
think I had things sorted out, but I've decided to see where
things lead. I hope I'm happy. I hope I'm the kind of person

*who figures it is better to do things and fail than regret
never having tried at all. I hope I have good friends and
have never forgotten Nora. I hope I'm in love with someone
who loves me back, and enough to give me the room to be
who I really am. It's scary not knowing, but it's also exciting.*

*I don't know what I'll be doing in ten years. Brody's
always talking about perspective. About if we change
how we look at things, we can see them in a new way.
I'm counting on seeing things differently when I'm out of
here. Maybe I'll be a writer. I might even have a kid of my
own. It's possible that Nora had the best plan way back in
first grade. She wanted to be a mermaid. I like that idea.
I hope I'm magical and free and unafraid of swimming
against the stream.*

I drew a mermaid at the bottom of the page. I wasn't going
to win any art awards, but I still liked it. I folded up the letter
and slid it into the envelope. Then I remembered something. I
pulled out my bag. I was still carrying around the photo Brody
had taken, the picture of the girl at the edge of the forest. I used
to think she was scared, that someone was about to eat her.
Now I realized she was at the verge of a big adventure. All she
had to do was turn around and face it.

I slid the photograph in with the letter and sealed it shut.
I glanced up. Brody had finished his letter and was waiting for
me. It was time to move on.

Want more Eileen Cook?
Read on:

It's not clear if Saint Thomas More had murder on his mind when he fell from his alcove in the north stairwell and onto my friend Win. It's far more likely that over the years the vibration of hundreds of high school students thundering up and down the stairs finally shook him free. The statue did a huge swan dive that would have made an Olympian proud and clipped Win right over her eyebrow. She caught him, saving the statue from crashing to the floor. It can be hard to help someone see the bright side of things when they are nearly taken out by a religious icon.

"Sod it all, I'm bleeding." Win looked at her face in the mirror above the nurse's sink. When Win was really ticked, she sounded even more like her British-born mom.

I handed Win a wet paper towel. "Look on the bright

side—saving a saint is going to earn you some valuable karma points."

"Harper, I'm not Catholic." Win winced as she pressed the towel to her forehead. "And it's not like I had a choice; the stupid thing basically fell into my arms. If it had been up any higher, it probably would have killed me."

"I can't see Tom holding your lack of religion against you." I leaned over and patted the plaster statue of the saint on the head as he sat innocently on the floor. Our school, Saint Francis, was one of the highest ranked in Washington State. This meant the student body was made up of people who wanted their kids to have a religious education and also those who didn't mind forcing their kids to wear the most hideous mustard-yellow and navy-blue uniforms ever created as long as they went to a good school. "Having a saint who owes you one is nothing to sneer at. You could club a seal or something and it still wouldn't be enough to land you eternal damnation."

"Stop trying to find the silver lining in every situation." Win squinted at her reflection. "Look at that: It's going to leave a scar. That's it. I'm disfigured."

"You're fine. The nurse doesn't even think you need stitches."

"She's a school nurse. Do you really think I'm going to leave the destiny of this face in her hands?" Win continued her self-inspection. Only she could get clocked by a statue and still look great. It would be annoying if she weren't my best friend.

"Fair enough. But you have to admit we got out of going to chemistry; you have to admit that counts as good luck," I pointed out.

"Seems to me you're the lucky one. You weren't nearly decapitated *and* you still got out of class."

The nurse bustled back into the room. She handed Win an ice pack. "You'll want to keep this on to reduce the swelling."

Win blinked. "Ice. Don't you think I should have a CT scan or something? I could have brain damage."

"You'd want an MRI," I said. "CT is more for orthopedic injuries."

Win shot me a look.

"It basically grazed you. The only part of the statue that hit you was the hand." The nurse pointed, and I saw that Saint Thomas More had lost a finger in the accident. It looked like his blessing days were over. I wonder if the finger would count as a holy relic if someone found it on the stairs. The nurse yanked a folder out of her desk. "You'll be fine. Just keep the ice on there." She scribbled something in the file and then glanced up at the clock. "You two are free to go. If you hustle, you won't be late for Friday assembly."

We were barely out of the door before Win said, in a voice loud enough to carry to the nurse, "If I die of a brain aneurysm, my dad will sue this place."

"Getting hit on the head won't give you an aneurysm," I pointed out as we moved down the hall. "They're usually caused by a weakness in the artery since birth. High blood pressure could cause one too."

"Having you as a friend is like having my own personal WebMD. Handy and terrifying all at the same time," Win said.

"You're welcome." Having a neuroscientist as a dad made me more knowledgeable on brain function than the average high school senior. It also meant that I was more likely to kick the bell curve's ass in anatomy.

We were among the last people to get to the auditorium, but the assembly hadn't started yet. My boyfriend, Josh, yelled out my name and waved us over.

I tugged on Win's arm. "He saved us seats." We moved down the row and plopped into our chairs. Josh squeezed my hand and I fought the urge to pull mine back. Josh was only happy when we were constantly touching.

"Heard God tried to take you down." Josh motioned toward the Band-Aid on Win's forehead.

"Ha-ha. Maybe as official class president you should figure out if any other parts of the building plan to crush a student. I'm no lawyer, but that seems like a lawsuit waiting to happen."

Josh saluted. "I'll get on that on at our next council meeting."

"It could have been worse—what if it had been that statue of Saint Sebastian in the cafeteria, the one with all the arrows? You would have lost an eye," I said.

"Thank you, Mary Poppins." Win grabbed gum out of her

bag and offered it to the both of us before jamming a piece in her mouth.

"It wouldn't kill you to see the positive side," Josh said.

"It might. Besides, that's why I keep her around." Win chomped on her gum with a smile.

We were unlikely friends. People called us yin and yang. She was half black; I was pasty white. I got nearly straight As, and she was happy with Cs. Win was the ultimate social butterfly, and I tended to be shy. Win vowed she wasn't going to be bothered with a relationship until she was at least forty, and I'd dated Josh for two years already. I always looked for the positive, and she had honed being cynical to an art form. There was no reason for us to get along, but we did.

Our principal, Mr. Lee, was on the stage waiting for everyone to pay attention. He did this sort of Zen thing where he would stand in silence with his eyes closed until we all shut up. You wouldn't think it would work, but it did.

"There's your dad," Josh whispered.

I followed his finger. My dad stood at the side of the stage, fussing with his tie. He almost never wore one. At work he got away with jeans, T-shirt, and lab coat. There are some benefits to owning your own company. Other than wealth and not having a boss, that is. I shifted in my seat. My dad liked to be goofy, which was bad enough at home, but I had no idea what he might pull at my school. I sent up a silent prayer that he didn't do one of his impressions.

"What's he doing here?" Win asked.

Saint Francis had a mandatory assembly every Friday with various speakers. The school promoted it as a chance for us to gather as a "community." "Community" sounded better than what we suspected, which was that the teachers liked having the last hour of the week free.

"He agreed to do a talk on the importance of science," I said.

Win pretended to snore.

"How can you say that? Science impacts everything," Josh said.

Win held up a hand. "Spare me. I'm going to have to hear the talk from her dad; I don't need to hear it from you, too." She flipped her hair over her shoulder. "Also, for the record, having a bromance with your girlfriend's dad is creepy."

Josh was ready to argue with her, but Mr. Lee was already introducing my dad, so we had to be quiet.

I'd heard Dad's science talk before. It was fairly interesting. He managed to connect all these major scientists like Darwin and Einstein to random things like punk rock and winning World War II. My prayer must have worked, because so far he'd managed to avoid doing any of his lame Dad stand-up comedy routine.

"Now, some of you know that my company, Neurotech, recently received approval from the FDA to offer our revolutionary Memtex treatment to teens and children." Dad stood with a Neurotech logo projected onto him and the screen behind him.

"Holy shit, we can go for a softening now?" someone hissed a few rows behind me.

I turned around to hear who had said that. My dad hated when people called it a softening. He thought it sounded too woo-woo. He was not a fan of anything that smacked of being new age.

"I thought you guys might like to be the first group to see our new commercial. Sort of like a movie screening, only without the hot movie stars—unless you count me." A few people laughed. It's a well-accepted truth that everyone else will find your parent's feeble attempts at humor funnier than you will. My dad spotted me in the crowd and waved. I scrunched further down in my seat.

The auditorium lights dimmed, and my dad stepped out of the glare of the projector. The commercial was well done. It showed a bunch of perfectly airbrushed teens in what adults must think of as ideal moments: dancing at a prom, laughing with friends over a bonfire on the beach, crossing the finish line at a track meet. No one had acne or bad hair. I recognized the main actress from some cable show.

"Are bad memories holding you back from doing everything you want and enjoying the life you deserve?" she asked. Her eyes stared out of the screen as if she personally felt bad for us. "You don't have to be bogged down anymore. Ask your doctor about

Memtex today—and imagine what you could accomplish tomorrow!" Her face split into a wide smile and just a hint of a wink.

The lights went up, and people applauded as if it had been an Oscar-winning performance. I wondered if Mr. Lee was ticked that my dad had managed to sneak a commercial into his talk. I could have told him he should have known better; my dad never missed a chance to promote his business. Once he slipped our dentist a brochure in the middle of a root canal.

"Well, thanks for having me today and letting me share with you why I find science so important, and how I think it can impact your life. I'm excited to have Neurotech providing services to teens. To mark that evolution in our company, I'm pleased to announce we'll be offering a part-time internship for a deserving high school student with a passion for the sciences. Applications are available on our website. At the end of the year the lucky recipient will also receive a grant to assist with college costs."

Josh jolted straight up in the chair next to me, vibrating with excitement. I couldn't believe my dad hadn't said a thing about this to me. He winked at me from the stage. That made me wonder what other surprises he had up his sleeve.

I can't believe you didn't say anything." Josh was practically bouncing off the lockers in the hall. He'd left being excited behind, had blown through thrilled, and was now hovering in an enraptured state. People who discovered they had a winning lotto ticket in their pocket were calmer than Josh at this moment.

"I told you, he didn't tell me anything about it." I grabbed my history and math books out of my locker. I smiled when I saw the picture of my horse, Harry, taped to the inside. Other girls might have pictures of hot actors hanging in their lockers, but I preferred Harry. He was arguably better looking, and certainly more loyal.

Win took the books out of my hands and put them back on the shelf. "You're not going to have any time. You have a riding lesson on Saturday. You know you'll end up spending the rest of the afternoon at the barn."

"That's Saturday. I can study on Sunday."

She shook her head. "You might think that, but Sunday is actually reserved for coming over to my place and hanging out. Enough with all the studying. Live a little."

"Do you have any idea how many applications they might get?" Josh acted like he hadn't heard a word we'd said. "It's a huge opportunity, but you'd have to be local. The job is here. I can't imagine anyone is going to let their kid move for an internship. That should cut down on the numbers. Plus, it's a short turnaround time. There are only a couple weeks to get an application together." He bounced on the balls of his feet.

"Chill out, Mr. President," Win said.

"Call me that, and I'll call you by your real name," Josh threatened.

Win's eyes narrowed. For reasons that eluded everyone, her otherwise cool parents had burdened her with her grandmother's name, Winifred. If you really wanted to piss her off, you would call her that. "Fine. Chill out, *Joshua*. My point is that you're a shoo-in for this internship. You're in the house of the guy who founded the entire freaking company almost every day. You're dating his darling daughter. Of course he's going to choose you. He probably came up with the program so he could give it to you while still making the whole thing tax deductible."

I made a point to roll my eyes as if I thought what she'd said was absurd. My stomach was in a tight knot. There *was* a chance he had come up with the program just for Josh. I was an only child, and it was pretty clear that my dad didn't know what to do with me. It wasn't that he didn't love me, but he didn't get me. My dad was into computer games, every tech gadget you could imagine, and boring science shows. Josh was the son my dad had always wanted. They liked the same movies, read the same science fiction books, and got each other's obscure jokes. They'd both been raised by single moms, had a passion for science, and were willing to work insanely hard for what they wanted.

It wasn't that my dad and I didn't get along, but they got along better. Josh made sense to him. I knew my dad worried about how Josh was going to afford college next year. Most of the time I liked that my dad and Josh got along, but lately it felt too close.

I grabbed my history book back out of my locker and stuffed it in my bag.

"If making out with the boss's daughter doesn't give you a better-than-average chance, what's the point of doing it?" Win teased him.

Josh leaned over and kissed me. "The point is I like making out with the boss's daughter. Even if she wasn't the boss's daughter."

"Hey, no PDA in the hallways." Win slapped the two of us apart. "You think I want to see that? I had a big lunch."

Josh made giant kissing noises near my face while Win pretended to gag. I did my best to ignore both of them.

"That's going to cause me trauma. Course now I can just soften that nightmare right out of my head," Win said.

"Memtex," Josh and I said in tandem.

"Thank you for the correction, groupthinkers. I can Memtex that vivid image out of my brain." She slung her Coach bag over her shoulder as we headed down the hall. "Don't you think it's a bit creepy? The whole 'dial down a memory that bugs you' thing."

"Are you kidding? Do you know how much Memtex has done for people with PTSD? The impact of past trauma is huge. The ability to . . ." Josh searched for the right word.

"Soften?" Win offered with a raised eyebrow.

Josh sighed. "Fine, the ability to *soften* those memories is a game changer."

"Look, I'm all for helping war vets or some crime victim move past what happened to them, but people go for treatment for everything now. Lose a job? Get a divorce? No problem, just soften the heck out of it until you don't care."

"For some people getting a divorce can be as traumatic as war," Josh said.

Win snorted. "Please. People need to ball up. Life isn't all sunshine and unicorns. Now they're selling it to people our age? What, because not getting into the college of our choice is crushing? No date for prom causing premature PTSD? It's not trauma; it's real life. Life is hard sometimes. It doesn't mean you don't face it."

"You realize the irony of you saying life is hard, don't you? You live in a house the size of a hotel and you spent your Christmas vacation in Venice."

"We didn't go to Venice," Win protested. "We went to Florence. Venice is too damp that time of year." She smirked at Josh. "I still stand by what I said: You have to learn to deal with life. Whatever it throws you, good or bad."

"But if you can make it easier, why shouldn't you?" I said. "Isn't that the point? Life is hard, but if there's a treatment that can make it less difficult so that you can focus on other stuff, positive stuff, that is dealing with it."

"And if you happen to run a pharmaceutical company, you can focus on making a few billion off the whole process." Win waved off what I was about to say. "Don't get me wrong. I'm for capital gains. Especially if it means we can use some of your dad's money to pay for a trip to Europe this summer before college. All I'm saying is that I wouldn't do it. No one is messing with this head." Win knocked on her skull.

"Don't mess with perfection?" I said sarcastically, as we walked toward the door.

"Exactly." Win stopped short after a few steps. She stared straight ahead. "Whoa."

I looked through the open front door. There was a crowd of people standing on the sidewalk. "What in the world?" I slid past her and closer to the door so I could see. Josh tried to grab my hand, but I stepped outside.

A group of about thirty protestors were milling around, holding signs. One said NO VOLUNTARY LOBOTOMIES; another said NEUROTECH—STAY OUT OF OUR CHILDREN'S HEADS! I drew back when I saw one woman in a neon-yellow tracksuit holding a sign that was a picture of my dad with a Hitler mustache drawn above his lip. NEURO-NAZI was printed in bright red letters underneath the photo.

"How did they even know your dad was here?" Josh whispered as we stood on the top steps of the school.

I scanned the front parking lot. My dad's car was gone. Company security must have whisked him out of there before the protestors arrived. The protests were getting worse if they were starting to follow him around. They usually stayed outside his office. No wonder he wanted to put a new security alarm on our house. "There may have been some kind of announcement on the company website that he was coming here for a talk."

"Or some eejit in this school tipped them off." Win scowled. "We should go."

"Who the hell do they think they are?" I asked. Didn't these people have jobs or someplace to be? Did they have nothing else to do but hang around yelling at people? I hated that they made me feel vaguely ashamed of what my dad did. "The treatment is voluntary. If they don't want it, no one is forcing them."

One of the protestors, a young woman in a business suit

with bright red lipstick, broke from the group and approached us. "Harper Bryne?"

"Oh, shit," Win said. "She knows who you are." Win grabbed my elbow and started to hustle me toward her car.

"I'm Lisa Gambel, a reporter, and I wondered if I could ask you a few questions." She pulled out her phone to record our conversation.

Win kept pulling me toward her SUV. "Don't talk to her. Whatever you say, she's going to twist it all around. Trust me, I've seen how they've turned around what my dad said in interviews, and they were sports reporters. God only knows what she'll cook up."

Josh walked behind me, shielding me from Lisa as we moved quickly. The pack of protestors swarmed around us, yelling to get my attention. I felt closed in. Why couldn't my dad do something boring like work in a bank?

"What are your thoughts on your dad's company offering the Memtex treatment to teens?" When I didn't respond, the reporter kept firing off questions without even pausing to let me answer. "Do you worry about the possible negative side effects? Have you heard rumors about serious complications? If there's even a chance of those complications, is it worth the risk?"

My heart raced. I knew the only reason they were hassling me was because they couldn't get a quote from my dad. The reporter wanted something in time for her deadline. She shoved the phone closer to me, and I pushed it aside. I wondered if this was how animals felt when they were being hunted, as if the world were collapsing around them. I stumbled on a loose piece of concrete, my foot catching in a pothole. I started to fall. Someone reached forward and grabbed me before I hit the ground, then pulled me up. He was tall and broad-shouldered, but loose-jointed and gawky, like one of those puppies that grew large before it knew what happened.

"You okay?" He held on to my elbow to make sure I had my balance. His touch was warm and chased away some of the chill. His eyes locked me into place, creating a focal point in the midst of all the screaming and noise.

I opened my mouth to thank him when I noticed he was wearing a T-shirt that said PEOPLE NOT CORPORATIONS! He was one of the protestors. Perfect.

"She's fine; please back off." Josh was at my side and guided me toward Win's giant SUV.

"Your father is a monster!" a woman yelled, inches from me. A fleck of her spit hit my cheek, and I recoiled.

The guy who had kept me from falling put a hand on the woman. "Hey, take it easy. She's not responsible for what her dad does."

His words hit me like a slap in the face. My fear sucked out like a wave, and in its absence rage rushed in. I lunged forward so that I was in his face. "I'm proud of my dad. At least he does something with his life. You think it's so easy to make the world a better place? Why don't you do something rather than bitch about what other people do?" I jammed my finger into his chest.

Josh wrapped his arm around my middle and pushed me into the open SUV door. Win was already behind the wheel. She gunned the engine, and it roared to life.

"Let's get out of here," she said.

Josh was right behind me, and he slammed the door. The silence inside the SUV seemed somehow louder than all the shouting outside.